FANTASIA ADVENTURES

PRIYANKHA KAMALAKANNAN

FOREWORD

As a teacher with over 11 years of experience with young learners, across different continents, I have seen several children put their creativity and imaginative skills into writing. While I value an individual child's capability, I can fearlessly say that the author (Priyankha Kamalakannan, 11 years old) is one of the most creative and talented writers I have ever met. Priyankha's commitment to writing is gaining global recognition, evidence which could be found on her ***TedxYouth Talk "The Power of Writing"***

The adventures and myths recorded in this book are ideally described, prompting real imagination and curiosity.

Welcome to Fantasia Adventures!

Lawrence Mayaki

2021

PROLOGUE

I sat with little Lizzie, who was playing around with my old books that she probably found in one of the dusty boxes. Lizzie caught sight of me and crawled onto my lap with a giggle. A few seconds later, she caught hold of my red ruby amulet. She rubbed my precious Amulet and stared into my eyes. At that very moment, I knew that Lizzie would follow in my footsteps, and become a great heroine, perhaps more powerful than me. I took off the amulet and fastened it around baby Lizzie's neck. There it sat, reflecting in the eyes of my little sunshine.

SOMETHING UNUSUAL

In a small cottage, on a farm in the English countryside, lived an ordinary family of four. John Thomas was a calm and hard-working farmer who started work early and finished late. His wife Rebecca was a busy woman and an expert at keeping everyday chaos under control.

They had two girls, one of whom was still quite young. The older child, ***Elizabeth***, often called ***Lizzie*** spent most of her time buried in a book about some sort of myth or legend. Lizzie was always to be found in different corners with a big, old book. She didn't care about what she wore, since she lived on a farm where things tended to get dirty. Most days she just stuck with plain blue overalls, black leather boots, and her hair in plaits. One of Lizzie's favorite things was her visits to her dear neighbor, Mrs. Browne. She often went over to Mrs. Browne to listen to her magical stories.

Mrs. Browne gave Lizzie a cinnamon bun every time she passed by. Lizzie's little sister, Annie, also came with her sometimes, but she didn't have much interest in myths and legends. Instead, each time Lizzie took her to Mrs. Browne's, she begged for a cinnamon bun.

Besides her frequent visits to Mrs. Browne, Lizzie preferred to be alone with books. On a particular day, her mind began to buzz with questions and ideas as she came across a page in one of her odd-looking books. It said, "If one is brave enough to venture the vast lands of Fantasia, one must accept the challenge of defeating the White Queen". Lizzie was intrigued. The message made a meaningless muddle in her mind.

Lizzie was puzzled by the message. What could the statement mean? Was this a cry of help? Or was it a message to her?

That same day Lizzie went over to Mrs. Browne's little cottage. As usual Mrs. Browne was ready with a sugary cinnamon bun, as Lizzie came in. She invited Lizzie over to the couch. Lizzie picked up her book and turned to the page with the puzzling message. She pointed with her index finger as Mrs. Browne read the fancy script out loud.

"Well, this is quite confusing, but I think that you'll understand quite soon enough," Mrs. Browne told her in her old, sore voice.

"I'm sure I will, Mrs. Browne! I'm quite excited for today's story" Lizzie agreed as she waited eagerly for Mrs. Browne to start telling her one of her magical stories. Mrs. Browne announced, "Today I will tell you the story of the White Queen".

THE WHITE QUEEN

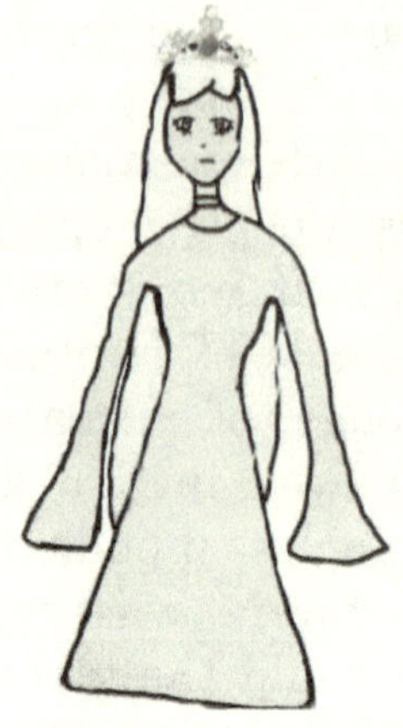

Once upon a time, there was a king who ruled the great kingdom of Fantasia. His citizens praised him for his good deeds. He also had a beautiful daughter called Sophie. She had the fairest, white skin and long, snowy white hair.

However, Sophie wasn't exactly a reflection of her father. She ordered servants around and demanded everyone to bow when she entered the room. When she went out to town, she rudely knocked over market stalls and snatched food and money. Soon this became too much for the creatures and people. A few representatives went to the king's court to file their complaints. The king was shocked.

He couldn't believe that his daughter had caused all of this. The king ordered Sophie to attend a court trial, and soon enough the judge proved her guilty. So, Sophie was sent to live in the dungeons of the palace, but on her birthday, she escaped from her prison cell and challenged her father to battle.

The king had no choice but to accept the duel. The ferocious battle was set to be on the day with the fullest moon of the month. At last, that very day came along, and both prepared themselves for battle. The king had assumed that the battle would be quite simple since it was against his weak daughter. However, Sophie proved him wrong. With all her might, Sophie lifted her sword and sliced her father's head clean off, savagely murdering him.

The death of the king meant that the reign of Queen Sophie, also known as the White Queen, had begun. That was the terrible fate that all of the creatures had feared, and now it was real.

* * *

"Now, I suppose this tale will help you on your quest. Hop along, it's time for supper!" said old Mrs. Browne.

Lizzie loved Mrs. Browne like her Gran. Lizzie's Gran had disappeared when she was still very young. Her Gran had left one thing for Lizzie, a very important thing. It was very precious and unique. It was her shiny, delicate ***ruby amulet***.

The amulet had a glittering golden frame, and it contained a beautiful and magnificent red ruby. Lizzie went to the drawer where she stored her most prized possessions. She picked up the amulet and fastened it around her neck as she was called for supper.

Mrs. Thomas had prepared a feast for that evening. On the table there lay glasses of milk, a bowl of hearty salad, a dish of creamy mashed potatoes, a pot with a colorful variety of veggies, a large plate of rice, and a juicy apple pie. Lizzie ate as quickly as she could because she wanted to read some more from her odd book.

Lizzie sat upright on her comfy bed and pulled the blankets over as she opened the heavy book, which had lain underneath her bed. Her eyelids felt heavy, but she continued to read anyway.

"The Realm of Fantasia" Lizzie read. "Fantasia is a place where all mythical creatures are united. Differences don't pull the magical beings apart; differences bring them together. The White Queen now rules Fantasia, wiping away most of its beauty, with her evil ways. The only hope for the Realm of Fantasia to be saved is if someone is brave enough to challenge the White Queen and defeat her for good to triumph over evil" she finished.

Lizzie stared at the page in shock. The White Queen was the evil Queen Sophie from the tale Mrs. Browne had told her! She sleepily continued to read.

"Fascinating Creatures in Fantasia. The realm has many intriguing...". Lizzie gradually closed her eyes and fell into a deep sleep that night...

Lizzie had a strange dream that night. She dreamt of being at Queen Sophie's palace, staring into her cold, grey eyes. All eyes were on her, for she was standing in front of the cruel Queen with people she didn't even know, and they each wore some sort of suit.

A tall, studious-looking boy with rounded glasses and an emerald green suit, a young cheery girl wearing a glamorous and glittery costume standing next to a seemingly average boy with clothing covered in amber-gold patterns and an older teenage girl covered in shiny blue scales, were Lizzie's companions.

Lizzie could hear excited cheers and shouts in the large crowds. Strangely, her Gran seemed to be there as well. Everyone who was there seemed to be cheering Lizzie and her companions on as if they were doing something good. Lizzie envisioned plenty of things in her dream, and as far as she knew, everything related to Fantasia and whatever she knew about the realm

However, the most troubling one of them all, was the vision of the White Queen herself.

THE ADVENTURE BEGINS

Lizzie woke up startled and gazed at the sandy beach in front of her. She rubbed her eyes and stared at the glistening water closely. Lizzie stood up and wandered around the unfamiliar place. Soon, she realized that she was not anywhere near the farm. Only then did Lizzie see the shiny ruby glinting on her neck. The amulet was with her the whole time! She began to suspect that there was something mysterious about the amulet.

Maybe it had brought her to this strange beach? She didn't know what had happened last night, after all.

Little fish were jumping in and out of the beautiful sea in front of Lizzie. She bent down to touch the grainy sand, as suddenly a colorful fishtail sprayed water on her. A beautiful face peeked out of the tall waves. Awestruck, Lizzie watched as the fish-like creature swam to the coast. It shouted something to Lizzie that she could barely make out. It gestured to Lizzie to enter the water, so she waded in with bare feet, holding up her long, blue nightgown so that it would not get soaked.

However, as she went in deeper and deeper, Lizzie started to change. Step by step, she turned into a creature looking like the one waiting for her ahead. Lizzie could now swim even faster, and she could even breathe underwater. Lizzie stopped for a moment to admire her shining turquoise fishtail and her now long and glossy hair, but the one thing that caught her eye was her red ruby amulet.

The amulet was the only thing that hadn't changed. It was still glittering color and colorful, fastened around her neck. Lizzie swam ahead with her speedy fishtail and soon reached the waiting creature. She swam up to the surface to take in the view from the middle of the sea. Soon, the enchanting creature came up to join her.

"It's a strange thing that you transformed to be one of us. I have never seen such a thing before. By the way, I am Coral, one of the mermaids of honor to the princess" the strange creature introduced itself.

Lizzie's mind started to put the pieces together. She had met a mermaid, and she had transformed into one. Lizzie knew only one place where all that could have happened. She had been somehow teleported to the realm of Fantasia!

Coral tugged at Lizzie's hand impatiently, because she wanted to take her to the underwater world of the mermaids.

Lizzie and Coral went down quite deep into the water. The further down they went, the more interesting it seemed to be. At first, Lizzie saw a few colorful corals. Next, she saw a large school of vibrant fish passing by. She also found a small shipwreck among the creatures.

After the stunning journey, Lizzie enjoyed the bustling town of the mermaids. It was filled with gorgeous nature, wonderful mermaids and mermen, and blissful chatter. Younger mermaids sped along paths to play games, making their parents laugh happily. mermen sat at beige-colored tables and enjoyed delicious oyster fries. This underwater town seemed as perfect as it could be.

As Coral led her along the crowded streets, they bumped into a pair of lookalike mermaids. The taller mermaid scolded Coral angrily before greeting her properly

"Hello Coral, who've you brought with you this time?"

Coral cheerily replied, "This is Lizzie, I found her wandering around at shore. She came for vacation from another place". The two other mermaids rudely glared at poor Lizzie, as Coral pulled her away.

Lizzie was honestly overwhelmed by all the wonders of the beautiful town. Curiously, she looked around as Coral tugged her past buildings and people. At last, she came to a halt and excitedly pointed at the structure in front of them. The fancy monument was covered with exquisite designs and large, golden pillars.

They entered the luxurious building together, as a mermaid wearing a truly exquisite shell necklace and holding a golden trident glided through the door.

"It's the Princess! Bow for her!" exclaimed Coral.

The Princess was very beautiful with fair skin, silky hair, and a perfect smile on her face. As the Princess spotted Coral and Lizzie amongst the crowd, she whispered something in Coral's ear and handed her an invitation.

Lizzie eyed the invitation closely and read "Princess Pearl invites you to her Grand Birthday Gala "

"Shhh! Not so loud!" whispered Coral.

She was clearly excited to attend. Coral continued "The Princess said that I could invite any other guest that I wanted to the gala! And I'm going to invite you!" she squealed.

"Me? But you barely know me!" Lizzie surprisedly replied.

"Oh, come on, you'll definitely enjoy it. Please?"

"Oh, all right, I suppose I'll tag along, but make sure that no one finds out about my real identity"

Coral promised to not give Lizzie away to anyone. The twosome strode along the sandy paths of the city down to the neighborhood where Coral and her family lived.

Coral's family home was a large cave lit up beautifully by fire lanterns. Shells adorned pretty much everything around the place. Coral's mother, Aqua was a very kind person who always cooked her soul out for anybody who visited. She baked delicious pearlweed pies and made juicy oysters.

Aqua's husband, Shore, was a gentleman who was a local musician and composer. As Lizzie ate a delicious feast made by Aqua, she listened to one of Shore's beautiful compositions. Shore sang about his wonderful home underneath the sea and the sea itself. Lizzie could see how much Shore loved his home under the water through his song. "Only if all songs could tell a story like this one," Lizzie thought to herself.

Coral suddenly came waltzing into the room. She twirled and turned around the place. Lizzie was baffled by Coral's dancing. Coral saw Lizzie looking at her perplexedly. "I'm just practicing a little bit for the gala. You didn't already forget, did you?" Coral explained, questioningly.

Lizzie had completely forgotten about the gala because she had been so focused on enjoying Aqua's food and Shore's music. Lizzie admitted sheepishly, scratching her head "Umm… yeah, I kind of forgot about the gala". Coral sighed, putting her hand on her forehead. Lizzie could see that Coral was a little stressed.

Lizzie reassured, "But don't worry, if we leave now, we can still get there on time and dance a little!". Coral rolled her eyes playfully, grinning mischievously. She took Lizzie by the arm and dragged her to the palace. They heard lots of excited chatter and energetic music. It was time for the gala…

AN OPPORTUNITY

Lizzie and Coral swam into the halls of the palace and stood in line to get their invitations checked by the guards. The guards were armed with shields and sharp spears, which made Lizzie feel scared. Her mind was buzzing with thoughts.

Would the frightening guards let her in? Would they find out who she really was? She wasn't sure. She would just have to wait and see.

Luckily, the guards nodded their heads when Lizzie showed them her invitation. Coral led her into a ballroom full of colorful décor and loud party music.

"Tadaaaa!" exclaimed Coral. Lizzie was awestruck.

"They must have needed a ton of people to do all this!" Lizzie said, surprised.

"Nope! All done by me!"

Lizzie continued to gaze at the exquisite setup, as she felt a hand on her shoulder.

She turned around only to see the Princess! "You must be Coral's guest! I'm Princess Pearl, the leader of the Underwater Kingdom! You can call me Pearl" Pearl greeted Lizzie, introducing herself.

"Yes, my name is Lizzie Thomas and Coral did invite me, but why did you come to talk to me? I mean, as a Princess wouldn't you have more important things to do?"

"I was at the shore this morning and I saw Coral take you to the mermaid town. I also saw you change into a mermaid from a normal girl. You didn't seem to be from anywhere around here, that's why I wanted to talk to you ".

Lizzie gulped. Would she be punished by Princess Pearl, the leader of the Underwater kingdom? Pearl just smiled and held Lizzie's hand. "Don't worry though, I won't tell anyone. I've seen this kind of transformation before" Pearl said soothingly. Lizzie was relieved. The Princess was a nice person after all.

Lizzie fiddled with her amulet. "I woke up on the seashore today. I don't know how I even got here! I think some sort of magic brought me here, but I don't know what!" she worriedly explained to Pearl. Pearl's expression changed suddenly. She stared unusually at Lizzie, puzzling her.

"Your amulet! I've seen it before! I think this is Betty's amulet!"

"Wait, Pearl, who is Betty and why did she have my amulet?"

"Lizzie, I am going to tell you a story, one that is known only in Fantasia. It is important that you know this so that you understand"

ELIZABETH THE BRAVE

Once upon a time, there was a very brave girl, called Elizabeth Thomas, but everyone called her Betty. None of the children in the neighborhood ever paid any attention to her, so Betty was always with her grandfather. Her grandfather always told Betty lots and lots of legends, myths, and tales, and the two would spend their remaining time marveling over new stories they found in old books. Betty and her grandfather had such an unforgettable bond over their mystical and magical tales.

Betty liked lots of the legends she and her grandfather had bonded over, but there was one legend that she loved most: The Legend of Fantasia. Betty received a red ruby set in an Amulet, as a gift from her grandfather who had found it on a trip to Scotland. She became very fond of it and was seen wearing it every day. Back then, the passage to Fantasia was still open, and once Betty found out about it, she decided that she needed to see for herself. So, she rode a horse to the forgotten forest, only to come across a tall tree.

However, that tree wasn't just any normal tree, it was a talking tree from the majestic realm of Fantasia. She approached the tree and suddenly, she landed on the Beach of Shells. Confused, she dived into the water, exploring the depths of beauty in the waters. It was then that I, Pearl, saw the beautiful amulet of hers. It was her belief that had let her enter the Realm of Fantasia.

Betty and I went on to become great friends, and we ventured all over Fantasia. Of course, the White Queen was not in complete control, otherwise, we would have been executed, if not, we would have been locked up in the dungeons of the palace. The both of us went on to support the King, and Betty even became the best advisor ever known to the King.

She and the King were the ones in charge of building the Museum of Fantasia. When Sophie became Queen, she wanted to knock down the museum, home to all of Fantasia's great history and most importantly, the Golden Staff. However, because Betty had such a strong love for the beautiful museum, she protested for the museum to stay, and Sophie ordered for her to be captured and killed at once.

She gave her life for the museum and therefore became known all over the Land. Betty was a great person, and all of Fantasia misses her greatly. She is now known as Elizabeth the Brave, having done the bravest of things for Fantasia.

* * *

Lizzie felt a strong connection between Betty and herself. It all suddenly clicked. "Pearl, my Gran was Betty Thomas!! She gave the amulet to my Mum and told her to give it to me when I was old enough! "Lizzie exclaimed in realization.

"I knew you two were related somehow!" Pearl announced triumphantly.

Just then Coral approached them and said "Hey Lizzie! You've found Pearl, I see"

"Actually, Coral, me and Lizzie were having an interesting conversation back here. We eventually discovered that Lizzie is related to Betty Thomas"

"You know, I miss her quite a lot, but Lizzie reminds me of her when we first met. Brown hair in plaits, smooth skin, and a lovely smile, oh, how good those times were"

"Anyway, Coral, you should be partying, not standing around at the back. Me and Pearl are going to finish our conversation and then we'll join you" Lizzie told her sternly.

Coral strode back to a group of young mermaids who were dancing to the jazz music that the Orchestra was playing.

Pearl looked around to see if no one was close to them. Once she was sure that they were alone, Pearl went up closer to Lizzie and started to talk to her in a whisper. "Lizzie, there is a secret group of creatures from Fantasia, who are working against the White Queen" she began.

"It would be great if you joined them, your Gran would be proud of you if you did, she always was trying to bring justice to Fantasia." Pearl continued.

"Pearl... I would love to, but how could I help if I have almost no knowledge about her?"

"Lizzie, nobody knows much about her. She is very secretive about everything, and there is only one person who knows her inside out. It was the White Queen's father, the King. Please, Lizzie. The more people who help, the better, even if someone doesn't know much. If you decide to join, the entire kingdom of Fantasia will be grateful to you, but just please make the right choice"

Lizzie thought for a few moments. She knew that Pearl was right. She had to do something. "Alright. If I join this group, I will share the information that I have, but I do need a way to go back to the farm. I have to do a few things before I can help out here" Lizzie explained.

"Of course, I will make sure that someone opens the portal to your home. Be ready to depart by tomorrow morning! Now, shall we go enjoy the night?" Pearl said with a broad grin on her face.

MYSTERIES

Lizzie slept in Coral's cozy room that night after the party and ate a marvelous breakfast that Aqua had prepared for her. Aqua was tearful and gave her a warm, tight hug before Lizzie left, since Shore and Coral had already left for work at Pearl's palace.

A merman called Hurricane took her to the portal, which lay deep beneath the Town. The Portal was hidden inside a dark cave and looked like a whirlpool. Hurricane gave Lizzie a bracelet and told her that it needed to stay on her wrist until she returned.

"You will know when the time comes to return, the bracelet will flash, and someone called Damien will appear," he said in his low, grim voice.

Poof!!! Hurricane was gone. Lizzie stepped into the portal, not knowing what lay before her.

Lizzie was dropped onto her bed as the door creaked open. She saw Annie peeking through a gap. Annie quietly crept in, climbed onto the bed, and sat next to Lizzie.

Lizzie cuddled her close, wishing that she could stay like this forever, but she knew she had to go back, to help save Fantasia, and make her Gran proud. After a while of dreaming alongside her sister, Lizzie realized that it was already morning and that she had been sitting with Annie for quite some time.

Lizzie hurriedly stood up, leaving her sister to sleep peacefully, and rushed to the breakfast table. Surprisingly, Mr. Thomas was still sitting at the table reading his newspaper.

"Why hello Lizzie, you're up early today. Want some toast?" he cheerily asked.

"Hello Dad, didn't know you were still here, why don't we enjoy some tea together?"

"Of course, take a seat!" Lizzie's Dad said through a mouthful of toast.

As Lizzie poured warm tea into two mugs, she questioned "Dad, did Gran tell you about her adventures in Fantasia?"

"Yes, she did, Lizzie. Your Gran spoke about some sort of magical creatures, beautiful landscapes, and a strange mermaid called Pearl. Of course, no one believed her, and I told her it was just a dream or something. Why such a sudden interest?"

"Oh, I don't know Dad, it just suddenly came to my mind. Wanted to know more…about my history I guess"

"Well Lizzie, if you would like to know more about our family history, maybe you should look at your Gran's collection of who-knows-what-books. Oh, don't forget to go visit Mrs. Browne, she will be expecting you" Lizzie's dad reminded her and stood up to brush off the crumbs on his shirt. He then picked up his axe and marched out of the house to get to work for the day.

Lizzie gulped down her tea and quickly got dressed. She picked up the old, odd-looking book she had read the night she landed in Fantasia and galloped over to Mrs. Browne's neighboring cottage. Mrs. Browne stood at the door as Lizzie approached, waving excitedly. She led Lizzie into the living room, which smelled like sweet cinnamon buns like usual. And true enough, there was a plate of sticky, warm cinnamon buns on the coffee table. Lizzie sat down and took a heavenly and gooey bun from the round plate.

After she finished her bun, Lizzie curiously asked "Mrs. Browne, do you know anything about Fantasia? Oh, also could you help me find some old photo albums in the attic?"

"Of course, my dear, I will help you. Any special reasons?"

"Can I let you in on a secret? You cannot tell ANYONE..." Lizzie whispered, trying to sound as secretive as possible.

"Oh, of course, dear, I have known you your whole life, and I love you as your Gran does. Old ladies like me can surely keep secrets!"

"I discovered that the White Queen is real! Her actions are crueler than they seem, and she's imprisoning hundreds of innocent creatures! However, there is a group of magical creatures, who are plotting against the Queen, and I'm going to help them"

"Well, I wonder where you found this out. Perhaps, from an old book you have?" Mrs. Browne asked curiously.

"I have a friend that told me about the group of creatures!"

"And may I know who this friend is?"

"I am sorry, but I am not going to be able to tell anyone that, not even you" Lizzie stated, loud and clear. She decided not to tell Mrs. Browne about Pearl, because she doubted her. Mrs. Browne shrugged at Lizzie as if to say, 'Your loss'.

"Anyways, I must be on my way. I'll go to the attic on my own! "Lizzie hurriedly said, rushing to leave the house as fast as possible. Mrs. Browne was behaving very suspiciously. Lizzie knew that she couldn't possibly trust her anymore.

When Lizzie reached home, Mrs. Thomas greeted her with a hug and a warm lunch of cabbage stew and toasted bread. The two had their lunch together and chatted for a while about the upcoming bonfire for Guy Fawkes Night. After a while, Mrs. Thomas stood up to wake Annie from her nap.

Meanwhile, Lizzie made her way back home to go up to the attic. To get to the attic, Lizzie needed to get the ladder from the pantry and use it to climb up to a trapdoor near her parents' bedroom. She picked up the ladder and walked over to the trapdoor. Lizzie leaned the ladder on the wall and climbed into the attic. Her Gran had also lived with them and had stored her old books in the attic. Lizzie had planned to find some photo albums and some of her Gran's books to bring back to Fantasia.

She dug through the piles of boxes in the cramped room, and surprisingly came to find a box labeled in large print with the words "Betty".

Lizzie stared at the box in awe. She just couldn't believe it. She had found something that was worth almost all of what her family had owned. Lizzie had found Gran's box of memories. She remembered Gran showing her some of the contents such as a tall, black staff with some sort of a red jewel on top or a shiny tiara, also including a jewel in the very middle. Lizzie held the staff carefully in both of her hands, examining the reddish crystal on top. There was something unusual about it, but she just didn't know what.

She decided to take the rest back to her bedroom for further examination. She was bubbling with excitement to explore the strange things.

Lizzie had just climbed out of the attic and was sitting in her bedroom. The box she had found earlier sat in front of her, eagerly waiting for her to open it. One by one Lizzie carefully removed the contents from the box. Among all the things she came across an odd-looking rope. It had an amber gemstone placed exactly in the middle of the handle, glinting in a ray of sunlight.

Lizzie picked up the rope to look closely. She wondered, what if it had been given to Gran? Maybe she had gotten it from Fantasia? Lizzie was surprised by the fact that her Gran had probably been involved in something else in Fantasia and she had never told her.

"How could Gran have ever kept something like this a secret? Why didn't she write a note or something for me?" Lizzie raged. All she could feel at that moment was anger. She was angry at her Gran, angry at Mrs. Browne, angry at almost everything.

Lizzie then checked her bracelet and realized that it was almost time for the person called Damien to show up. She quickly gathered her book, the rope she had found, the staff, and a change of clothes in a satchel.

Soon enough, her bracelet flashed and before her eyes stood Damien. Well, to Lizzie's surprise, Damien wasn't exactly how she had expected him to be, to be honest, he was a lot bigger. He towered over the little cottage and was taller than one of the fruit trees nearby.

His voice thundered "Well, Hello Lizzie! I am sure that you must know my name already, Damien. I will be bringing you to your first meeting with the Society of Justice, a group of members who fight for the rights of all living creatures".

Lizzie's jaw dropped. She had never imagined that Damien would be this large and would have such a loud thundering voice! She frightenedly replied, "Erm...yes. I'm Lizzie and I have heard about you. The Society of Justice sounds quite interesting, and I am honored to join!".

"No need to fear me, I'm just a friendly giant. It's wonderful that you would love to join the society, they need more backup" Damien thoughtfully exclaimed.

"Well, that's a relief. Let's get going!"

Damien started taking large, heavy steps, whereas Lizzie had to run very fast to keep up. Damien turned around, picked up Lizzie, and dropped her into his shirt pocket. Lizzie looked at the large fields in front of them. Children from all cottages were playing Jacks, a common neighborhood game for children. To play the game, you would need ten small pebbles and one medium-sized rock. To win a pebble, you would throw the rock in the air, quickly pick up a pebble and catch the falling rock. The game ended when all pebbles were gone, and whoever had the most pebbles would win.

Lizzie badly missed watching those fun neighborhood games, as she used to do while she was reading. But she was out on a mission to save Fantasia. Damien had brought her to the Forbidden Forest, where the Old Portal once stood.

"The portal here doesn't work anymore, why did we come here?" Lizzie puzzledly asked.

"Ah, but there is a hidden portal in the depths of this forest, which will take us to the location of the Headquarters of the Just Soc"

The two wandered deep into the forest until at last, they had reached a small stream. Damien bent down to get a drink of water, forgetting about Lizzie in his shirt pocket. Lizzie flipped into the stream and almost got pulled away by the current, but she held onto a nearby rock with all her might. Damien quickly lifted Lizzie out of the stream and put her back in his shirt pocket. He reached out to a nearby branch and pulled off a leaf. Suddenly, a large, round hole appeared, and Damien stepped into it along with Lizzie, disappearing to another dimension...

A MISSION

Lizzie woke to find herself on a cozy mattress. However, the mattress seemed to be quite large. She crawled around on it, trying to jump off, but it was too high.

"Why is everything so large here?" Lizzie wondered out loud. At that very moment, Damien and a strange-looking creature entered the room. "Aha! I see you woke up! Welcome to the Land of Giants, Lizzie!" Damien welcomed her.

"So that explains why everything is huge here!"

"Yes, since you are in the land of giants, everything will be much larger than normal"

"And who is your friend?" Lizzie asked, pointing toward the strange creature who had entered the room along with Damien. "Oh sorry, I forgot to introduce her to you! This is Flutter, a pixie who works with the Just Soc. She will be accompanying you to the headquarters"

"I see. Hello Flutter! I'm Lizzie, but I think you already know that. Anyway, when do we have to go to headquarters?"

"We will leave for the HQ in 30 minutes, so you better get ready. I hope you brought a change of clothes because we won't be able to get you clothing for a while. We will be waiting at the breakfast table, where we all will have some breakfast. Be down in 10 minutes!" Flutter instructed Lizzie.

Lizzie stepped into some fresh clothes and walked out of the large room. She was going to run down the staircase, but it was far too high. She saw a railing and decided to slide down. Lizzie climbed up the metal bars and slid down, landing on the floor with a thump.

Suddenly, she saw Damien coming down the staircase, waving at her wildly. "I thought you wouldn't be able to make it down the stairs. Thank goodness you did!"

He picked up Lizzie and brought her to the breakfast table. On the table there lay a magnificent feast of crunchy toast, sweet jam and marmalade, a variety of cheeses, fruit, milk, and juice. Some of the plates were quite large, whereas others were smaller, suitable for Lizzie and Flutter. Lizzie grabbed her plate and tried to take a slice of cheese, but it was too heavy for her.

Damien had to put everything on the plates for Lizzie and Flutter. By the time they had finished one slice of cheese, some toast with marmalade and a small glass of milk. Lizzie was quite full of food, but she got up anyway. Damien waved goodbye to them as Flutter led Lizzie out of the house and along a path to a cart station. They sat down waiting for the cart chain to arrive. Finally, it arrived, and they all hopped on. The magical cart chain was on the road for about half an hour or so. Once Flutter and Lizzie had jumped out of the cart, they set out into the city of Downtown.

The city of Downtown was bustling with creatures of all kinds and there were many tall buildings. Most people in the city were quite friendly and they were always up for some fun. The trio pushed through the crowds and at some point, they finally reached the HQ. The HQ was an ordinary-looking building with large glass windows and big rectangular doors. Lots of people were coming in and out of the building. Lizzie was excited to find out what awaited her.

Flutter and Lizzie entered through one of the large doors, not knowing what to expect. Inside the building, people were lining up at the reception with tall stacks of paper. They climbed up the large stairs and entered a room labeled 'Conference Room'. There was a large, round table that had enough seating for around twenty-five people.

Suddenly, a tall, strange-looking woman appeared in the room. She happened to be Pearl, but she had just morphed into a human. Was this how she attended meetings such as this one? "Hi, Pearl! How are you today?"

Pearl turned around to see Lizzie. "Shh, Lizzie you mustn't be loud around here. Alexa doesn't like it. Don't ask any questions, they will be answered later. Now, please go and take a seat at the table and be as quiet as possible" Pearl whispered, calmly telling Lizzie what to do.

Flutter and Lizzie sat next to each other at the large, round table. One by one, people began to file in and sit down. After a while, everybody had been seated and they were waiting for the leader of the operation.

The door creaked open and there she was. Click, clack, click, clack went the heels of the shoes of Alexa Nobleheart, the leader of the Just Soc as she walked in. She eyed each creature at the round table. Alexa sat down at the last empty chair, pulled out a piece of a map and laid it on the middle of the table. She looked at a few people as though she was waiting for them to do something, but she then followed the direction of their gaze, directly at Lizzie and stopped staring at them.

"Ahem... we have a new member joining us today. Elizabeth Thomas, whose ancestor was Betty Thomas, the great heroine famous in Fantasia for saving our history. Many creatures started to murmur. Lizzie, my name is Alexa Nobleheart, if you don't know. Pearl will answer your questions at your table later." Alexa began.

"Now we must work on finding the nearest route to receive information about Sophie. I hope you all know who that is. But before we do that, does anyone have any evidence for information? If so, please come to me after you are split into your teams"

Everyone pushed their chairs in and walked over to separate tables. Lizzie had her book that she wanted to show Alexa Nobleheart, so she remained seated. Surprisingly, Lizzie was the only one still sitting. She opened her satchel and pulled out the large, old book to show Alexa. She opened it to the page with the mysterious message and pointed at the small text for Alexa to see. Alexa was wearing her reading glasses, trying to read the bitty, neat writing.

Alexa agreed "Indeed, this is very strange. We must do some further investigation. I shall copy down this message and come back to you with any results. Do you have any information or thoughts about this statement?"

"Well Alexa, I do feel like this message is addressed to me. However, I don't have any other thoughts or information about it"

"I shall update the system about this issue. Thank you for sharing, Lizzie. You will be with Flutter, Pearl, and a few others today"

Lizzie gathered her things and quickly walked over to her table. She pulled up a chair and sat down next to Flutter. "Hi everyone, since we all don't know each other yet, why don't we do an introduction circle? We have exactly five people, that's the perfect amount!" Lizzie exclaimed.

"Well, I think that's perfectly fine with me and everyone else. Why don't we start with you?" replied a short, fat man.

"I'm Lizzie Thomas, and I'm excited to be working with you"

"I'm Pearl, and I am the leader of this group"

"Flutter here, and I work on disguise and camouflage for operations"

"Ahem, my name is Dwarfer, and I record information" the short, fat man introduced.

"Finally, I'm Branch, and I can morph from a talking tree into a human" the last person quietly introduced.

"Great! Now we have some background knowledge about each other. Let's get started!" Lizzie enthusiastically exclaimed.

Pearl opened a box that contained a large stack of paper and grabbed the top three. “We need access to the Queen’s office files, which she has on her computers in a room in the forbidden hallways. We have to find evidence as for when we try to accuse her. So far, we have not done much for our task, so let’s try to step it up. We’ll meet at the giant’s inn tomorrow afternoon to work on our task, Got it?” Pearl instructed. Everybody nodded. It was on. It was time to get to work.

CLUES

The next morning as Lizzie and Flutter woke up in the giant's inn, Damien had cleaned all rooms and was waiting downstairs for them with another large but delicious breakfast. The two wearily jumped down the stairs for breakfast with Damien. All three of them munched down toast and marmalade. Lizzie was quite impatient because she wanted the afternoon to come fast.

At last, the afternoon came, and Pearl was the first one there. She loudly knocked on the door. "Knock, knock, KNOCK!!! Damien opened the heavy wooden door for Pearl as she waltzed into the inn. "Why hello again Pearl! Long time no see!" Damien chuckled. Pearl smiled and started to set up the table they would be working at.

Next came Branch, who must have knocked at least ten times before she was heard. She looked quite bored as she entered the room, and she was nowhere near happy to see the others. Branch placed herself next to Pearl at the table uncomfortably, while Pearl herself was busy organizing the materials for their project.

Dwarfer arrived quite late, but he was the one who had to run all the way from the other side of Town. "Huff...huff...huff! I am tired, so let's get this over with" an out-of-breath Dwarfer wheezed. He, too, sat down on one of the hard chairs next to Pearl.

As soon as everybody was seated, Pearl began her explanation of the day's task. "Good afternoon everyone! Today's meeting will start with a session on route-making and later, the discussion of tools. All understood?"

"Let's begin with a few maps. These will help us find a good route to reach the Queen's palace. Remember, the Queen has lots of people who can tell her about anything suspicious, so choose your route wisely. In the end, we should all meet up at the same place, the palace Gardens. Your task is to draw your own map of portals and to draw your route on that map. Shall we start working?" she finished.

Lizzie had literally no clue about the maps she picked up. She didn't understand them, she couldn't read them, or she couldn't use them. Instead, she just stared at one of the large parchment maps in front of her. When Pearl came by to look at Lizzie's work, she pretended to investigate one of the maps. "Pretending to be able to read those, are you? Well, why don't you just ask for some help?

"Uhh...yes, I might need some help with this map. That would be great!"

The two worked together, reading the maps, and noting down their route on parchment. Lizzie drew the streets, alleyways, and portals on their rather small parchment as Pearl read out coordinates and names of stations. Once they finished their map, they examined it one last time to make sure it was perfect.

The other three gradually finished their maps and gathered around the round table. One by one, each person shared their route with the team. Pearl nodded approvingly at every route, trusting that it would lead to their meeting point.

"All right, now that we finished our routes, we will be moving on to the next step for today, which is our resources. We need to make sure to bring the right things for our mission. So, it's time to make a list of requirements. Ok, let's begin" Pearl said, clapping her hands excitedly

The team talked it over for a while and eventually came up with a list of necessary items. Lizzie wrote everything down so she wouldn't forget a single thing. It was a bit of a long list, but they did need quite a lot of things to be able to secretly access the Queen's computer files. Since Lizzie was taking the same route as Pearl, they split the materials between them. Each person had to bring their own clothing of course. But other things could be split up.

The team decided to take a break from work and had some food. Damien brought ooey-gooey cinnamon buns, a plate loaded with fries, and tall glasses filled with punch. "Dig in!" encouraged Damien. Branch didn't eat much, Lizzie thought she was on a diet. Pearl dived for the cinnamon buns and bumped into Lizzie, who was already grabbing as much as she could. Flutter had a little of each, and she was eating quite slowly. However, Dwarfer had loads of fries and cinnamon buns. He squirted gigantic blobs of ketchup onto his already-full plate.

"What on earth are you doing? How would you be able to eat that much! You are going to waste a lot of food, and that is a crime!" Branch shrieked.

Dwarfer just shrugged and started to put a handful of fries into his mouth. Then he put in another, and another, and another. By the time he ate six handfuls, all the fries on his plates were finished. Next, he went for the delicious cinnamon buns, stuffing them one by one into his mouth. After just a few minutes, he had already finished everything on his plate, whilst everybody else hadn't even finished half.

"Now do you believe I'm wasting any food? Not every small creature has a small appetite"

"Uh...not really. I'll just finish what I have" Branch backed away. The other four chuckled. Finally, everybody had finished eating and cleaned off their plates. Branch and Dwarfer had mentioned they needed to leave, so they left right after. Flutter had planned to go into town to the markets, so she left with them.

Only Pearl and Lizzie were left with Damien. Pearl and Damien chatted for a while, as Lizzie climbed up the stairs to read her book. She jumped onto the large bed and pulled open the book. She came across a page, titled "The White Queen". "Queen Sophie, the cruelest heir to Fantasia's throne, shares nothing with anyone. The Queen keeps all her secret information using a special application on her computers. This was discovered by Betty Thomas, former advisor to the King" the book showed. Lizzie's mind was whirring. "If we access Queen Sophie's secret files, we will be able to stop the Queen's plans and we might be able to end her reign!" Lizzie thought. She needed to tell Pearl about her idea instantly.

Lizzie rode down the railing and bumped onto the floor. She ran into the dining room and waved her hands wildly in the air, jumping up and down. Damien picked her up and placed her on the table "Anything new?" he asked.

"Yes!!! Where is Pearl? I have a new idea! She has to know about it right now" Lizzie hurriedly told.

"Hold on kiddo, she'll be right back. Pearl went to find some of the necessary materials for your trip"

"Oh! There she is!" Damien exclaimed as Pearl came in with a large, heavy bag.

"Hey Pearl! I just came up with a great idea. Want to hear it?"

"Hello, Lizzie! Of course, why not? It might just help us with the mission"

Lizzie opened the big old book and showed the page she had seen earlier to Pearl. Pearl stood there for a while, thinking quite deeply.

"Is your idea to transfer almost all of Queen Sophie's data to our data storage, so we have access to her plans all the time? If so, that is one great idea. With that information, we can be one step ahead of her so that we can overthrow the Queen and end her reign!" Pearl came to the point.

Lizzie excitedly nodded and clapped her hands. "This is exactly what I thought of! I think this will help us a lot in our mission, don't you think so too?"

"Yes, that's right. This idea will help us enormously in our mission. Let's implement this strategy, but we mustn't let anybody know. They might spread this to others, eventually leading to Alexa. You know how Alexa is"

The two began to plan how they would get access to all of Queen Sophie's information. They also needed to keep this a secret from the others, but they knew they could do it. Pearl left after a while of work, and Lizzie had dinner with Damien. Strangely, Flutter was not back yet from the market. What could have happened? Lizzie didn't know. Neither did Damien. They planned to get a good night's sleep and try to find Flutter in the morning.

PLAN TO DESTROY

When the two woke up the next morning it was a cloudy rainy day. Damien had prepared quite an appetizing breakfast, but for some reason, nobody was hungry. Lizzie and Damien got dressed and took umbrellas with them to protect themselves from the rain.

Damien led Lizzie to the large markets downtown and showed her around the place. Damien knew every shop and he also knew exactly which shops Flutter would normally go to. Lizzie skipped along with Damien as he asked store owners if they had seen Flutter the previous day. But none of them had seen her. Some said she didn't even come to the market. Damien and Lizzie knew there was something fishy going on.

Damien decided to take Lizzie through the market to explore. Lizzie showed interest in the brightly colored clothes sold by tailors and the delicious tasting street food made right in front of them. Damien bought her some of the delicious treats and some brightly colored clothes, as a sort of souvenir for her time at the inn.

The two hopped onto a cart back to the inn. They knew they were unsuccessful in trying to find Flutter, but they hoped she would turn up soon. Damien told Lizzie not to worry and to just go to sleep. Pearl would know about this tomorrow.

By the time Lizzie woke up the next day, Pearl had arrived and was sitting at the table with Damien. Lizzie waved at Pearl politely. But Pearl only gestured for Lizzie to come down. Lizzie took a seat at the round table and Pearl asked "What happened? How did Flutter disappear so suddenly?".

"I haven't a clue. I haven't lived with Flutter for so long. Ask Damien, maybe he knows" Lizzie angrily replied, stomping back upstairs.

Damien and Pearl chatted a little more downstairs. Lizzie's head had been hurting for a while. So, she decided to lie down on the comfy bed. Lizzie napped for a while and dreamt happily. Sleep did her some good.

Lizzie woke up after a few hours and went downstairs. Pearl had left and Damien had laid out a delicious-looking dinner for her. She sadly munched down the dinner, wishing that she hadn't been angry at Pearl. There wasn't much left for her to do, so she just went to bed. She had to get some rest before tomorrow's team meeting at HQ.

Lizzie wasn't happy to see Alexa Nobleheart again. To be honest, Lizzie could have thrown her into the seas, feeling awesome afterward. She knew if she did that she would be in big trouble. She took her place at the table beside Flutter's empty chair. Soon, all chairs had been filled up except for Flutter's.

Click, clack, click, clack, went the heels of Alexa's shoes. She announced "Hello, members of the Just Soc. It seems that today we have a member missing. Has anybody seen Flutter?

"Not at all. A few people have asked around the place Flutter was supposed to be. But nobody had seen her" Pearl reported.

"Very well. We must continue with our mission. As I see no one has anything to report, we will just carry-on working. I hope you have been planning these past few days. You know what to do, any evidence, stay here. Begin!" Alexa ordered.

Pearl and Lizzie were the only ones still seated. They looked at each other, wondering what Alexa would say.

"You again. What now?" she scowled.

"Remember the book I showed you last time? There is a page with some information, which possibly might be useful to us" Lizzie tensely spoke, hoping she would be believed.

"Yes, go on..." Alexa said, nodding approvingly.

"Well, if you look at the page titled 'The White Queen', it says, Queen Sophie, the cruelest heir to Fantasia's throne, keeps almost everything unknown to all. The Queen keeps her information on a special application on her computers. This was discovered by Betty Thomas, former advisor to the King"

"What do you want to do about that?"

"This information has given us an idea. We plan to access the computer files of the White Queen, transfer the data system to the Just Soc computers and use the information we receive about her plans to overthrow her" Pearl explained.

"I see. I suppose you haven't told your team about this, am I right?". Pearl and Lizzie shook their heads.

Alexa sighed. "Alright, the idea is nice, but it's quite a hard plan to implement. Why not just take the easy way and win without any risk?"

"This way allows us to complete the process faster, and this causes permanent damage to the Queen. Yes, it is a bit risky, but it makes a much better impact!" Pearl argued.

"Damage to the QUEEN! She will imprison us, even worse murder us! Don't even think about it"

Lizzie started to think. What Alexa had said, had only made it a bigger reason to damage the Queen. She whispered to Pearl "Do you think we could do permanent damage to Sophie without Alexa?".

"In your dreams Lizzie! She has a bunch of minions who would instantly discover us" Pearl snorted.

"But remember Pearl, you need to make your dreams a reality, if you want better for you and the world. Let's do it Pearl. Do it for Fantasia".

"Oh, alright Lizzie. I'll do it for Fantasia. For Betty. But in the first place, how are we going to do this alone?"

"We probably need to spread the word around, most people don't like Alexa. They will hopefully help us"

Lizzie and Pearl sat at their team's table, where Branch and Dwarfer waited for them. They talked for a while about Flutter's disappearance.

Lizzie began to tell them about the idea she and Pearl had come up with. Branch and Dwarfer were a bit unsure at first, but after Lizzie explained they were all enthusiastic about the idea. The team split up and decided to inform the others. All the others were on board with the idea. They hated Alexa's ego. The Just Soc decided to meet the next day, without Alexa, at a special place called The Traveler's Café. Pearl, Lizzie, Dwarfer, and Branch cheerily walked together to the inn to prepare for the next day, since they were the mission leads.

Pearl prepared a list of tasks to operate the mission. There needed to be some people tracking the information from Queen Sophie's files, people organizing resources, a few people to distract Alexa so that she wouldn't get wind of their plan, and a few people to go to the palace and access Queen Sophie's secret files. "There is a lot to be done. But this is all for justice. Let's make our efforts worth it!" Lizzie exclaimed.

The small group was all packed up and ready the next morning as they stepped out of the cart to find the Travelers Café. After a while looking around, they eventually found it and went inside. They picked out a large big table enough to seat around 25 people. Soon the small groups one by one filed in through the door and took their seats. Everyone ordered something to drink or eat, choosing local Giant Town specialties.

Once all other customers had left, the owner himself left the building and closed the door. A "**WE ARE CLOSED**" sign was put upon the door. Pearl and Lizzie stood up to begin.

"Hello, we are Pearl and Lizzie, the operation leaders. Today we would like to assign a few people to each task, which will help enormously in the mission. But before we start, we need you to be sure that none of you will give this secret operation away. I think you all agree, so let's begin. So far, we have these tasks: resource organization, monitoring and distracting Alexa, tracking data from palace servers and we, the mission leads, will go to get access to Queen Sophie's files. Any changes?" the operation leads instructed.

"Your plan is nothing but the best. I think this is a great idea for an organization. After all, we do want each team to do something" a tall, skinny man remarked. Every other team agreed with this decision.

"Ok, so now that we have all assignments confirmed, we need to have time and a place to meet to discuss the status of our operation. At HQ meetings you must remember to pretend to work on your tasks assigned by Alexa. We can't have her find out, or else she'll probably stop us from carrying out our plan. Now you are going to meet with your team members and find out the timeline for your part of the mission. The operation leaders will come to each team to find out the timeline so they can coordinate the mission accordingly. Understood?" Dwarfer explained.

After a while, the team leaders had gone to each table and were now planning the overall timeline of the mission. "The sooner we find the Queen's secret files, the faster we end the White Queen's reign" Branch said as the meeting closed.

"We will be meeting at the same time, same place tomorrow. The operation has just begun".

IN ACTION

Over the following days, the teams met daily at the Travelers Café. The mission leaders had decided to begin the operation in just one week, so they had to be fast on their feet. The file transfer device was being prepared, the resources for traveling were being packed, distractions were being prepared for Alexa and people were getting ready to invade the palace of the White Queen.

The group working on the tech side of the operation, who met up regularly at the Traveler's Café, planned to create and keep the file receiver in its basement. The owner of the Café was an uncle of Lora, who was part of the group working on the receiver, so they were free to come over any time. Setting up their system took a lot of time though, and they needed much more help than they thought.

Lora was walking around in the marketplace when she saw Cooper, a member of the resource team, walking around with nothing to do. She waved at him, and he came over to talk to her. As they chatted for a while about how their part of the mission was going as an idea struck Lora's mind. She could ask Cooper and his friends for help! Then the file receiver would be ready in time for Lizzie and the others to be able to send a copy of the Queen's secret files! She asked Cooper if they could come over to the Café today to help and fortunately, he had time and said yes! So from that afternoon onwards the two groups worked together hard on the file receiver.

Cooper's group, who had packed resources for Lizzie and the others, met in the marketplace to buy the necessary items on the list. They had tried hard not to get noticed by any giants who knew them, but they couldn't avoid getting into conversation with the shopkeepers, some of which slowed them down. However, in the end, they managed to find whatever they needed, and they were done packing resources after a few days.

The others were busy making silly distractions for Alexa Nobleheart. They came up with fake evidence to show at meetings, long speeches to delay her, and even sleepy cakes, which were supposed to make her fall asleep. They tested these ideas out on Damien in the inn. The results were quite hilarious, and every evening when Lizzie came home, she always had something to entertain her.

At the same time, Lizzie and the others were making plans for their trip to the palace. They decided that Branch would stay behind to look out for Flutter. After all, she was part of their group. Pearl and Lizzie checked in on the other teams to see if they were ready to start the operation. They received their bags from Cooper and his friends, checked the data receiving system set up by Lora, Cooper, and the rest of their team, and checked the results of the tested distractions made by the final group. Finally, they were ready. The mission could begin. But before the mission could start, they had to attend the meeting at HQ. Each team walked into the meeting room and silently took their places. “Click, Clack, Click, Clack" went the heels of the Alexa Nobleheart’s shoes

"I see you are all present today, except for Flutter. Today we will do a bit of planning and then we will meet again, to track our progress. Begin!" she barked. Two members from the distraction group stayed back at the table, with fake evidence. Their group had crafted a couple of realistic keys that were meant to be used to open a chest nearby. They showed Alexa, and soon she had grabbed the keys and darted out of the room.

Everyone was in a jolly mood; they worked on their mission and enjoyed the time that Alexa was gone for. Eventually, the meeting ended, and everyone had left the room. Alexa came back the next day, thinking that all the team was still there. But she was wrong. She had spent a whole day searching for a treasure that didn't even exist. Alexa, recognizing her foolishness, decided to play a little trick of her own.

A few days later, over the weekend all four groups met at the Travelers Café to celebrate the success of their trick. However, Alexa followed them to the café and pulled out a key. This was the key to the café. No one knew about the fact that Alexa had locked up the operation team in the café.

After a while of eating and chatting, Cooper stood up and started to dance. A few minutes later, others from his group joined him on the dance floor. The music was running loud from a boombox someone had brought along. Dwarfer dragged Pearl and Lizzie down to the party because they were just sitting still and staring at everybody else.

Branch was in the center of the party dancing her heart out. The music kept changing and kept getting louder. The teams danced for hours and hours until they got tired. When Pearl checked the time on the clock, she was astonished. It had turned to 10pm already! Pearl gathered everyone and told them it was time to go. Lizzie ran to open the door, but surprisingly, it was locked! Pearl came over and tried opening the door as well, but still didn't open.

Lora started to cry. "How could my uncle have done this to us! Why would he!" she wailed.

"I am sure your uncle didn't do this. It must be someone who wants to get revenge on us" Pearl reassured her.

"What if Alexa locked us up? She might want to get revenge on us for sending her on a search for fake treasure" Dwarfer pointed out.

The more they thought about it, the more sense it made. Alexa was the kind of person who would get revenge on others. However, they first needed to concentrate on getting out of the café.

Each team looked around to find a way to escape but they seemed to be stuck. The entire group crept around the rooms of the café finding materials to help them survive the long night. The resource team quickly sewed together a few blankets for everyone to sleep in. The tech team tried to figure out how to unlock the door. The group, which was distracting Alexa from their mission, made large batches of pies for a late dinner. Meanwhile, Lizzie, Pearl, Dwarfer, and Branch were investigating the café.

Pearl led Lizzie, Dwarfer, and Branch to the basement storage of the café. There were many rooms, but the room that caught their eye was the room labeled "Papers". What kind of papers could they be? Lizzie thought. Lizzie and the team decided to search through this room to look for evidence.

The room was unexpectedly large, filled with heavy cardboard boxes. Each box had a label, all except for one. It was a black box, standing alone at the corner of the room. While the others poked around in the remaining boxes. Lizzie lifted the lid from the box and picked up the first piece of paper.

"Map of the palace valley" she read. Lizzie looked closer at the paper and revealed a detailed map of the popular valley. She looked at the beautiful valley and the palace of Queen Sophie. The palace was large. Much larger than any other part of the valley. Lizzie was astonished. This would definitely help them in their voyage to Queen Sophie's palace. She rushed to go to show Pearl and the others. They, too, were surprised by the map.

The group wanted to bring the map upstairs to show the others. When they got back, they saw that everyone had fallen asleep. The team sat down with their blankets for a while, and eventually, they too fell into a deep sleep.

The next morning, all the teams woke up to the sound of Lora's uncle shouting at them. "What are you still doing here?".

The group stood up, relieved and explained their night at the café to him.

"That Alexa Nobleheart isn't so noble as her name says. She is nothing but a mischief making liar" Lora's uncle spat.

"How do you know her?" they politely asked.

"Well, we both started the Just Soc back in the old days and we were great friends, but that was only until I found out about her secret doings. Alexa lied. She knew I wouldn't like what she did, and she was darn right. Alexa started working for the Queen, secretly passing on information from the Just Soc and in return, she was given gold. After a while, she missed a lot many meetings and I decided to get to the bottom of it. I interviewed her family, friends, and even her employer, but none of them knew. I had to ask Alexa herself. She confessed and begged, pleading that she was sorry. But I knew, I could never work for a person who betrayed me. I left her, the group and my friends to start a new life. However, I never have forgotten our friendship. I still keep a picture of us, in my pocket watch, to remember the good times we had as Alexa and Dan", Dan sadly explained.

Everyone felt sorry for Dan, even Lora, who herself hadn't heard the story before. Dan told them to leave, although they wanted to talk to him, so the group left and went back to their homes while Lizzie went back to the inn.

THE JOURNEY BEGINS

Days had passed since the entire group had met. Lizzie went on about her daily life at the inn, sweeping the floors, dusting the shelves, etc. Flutter was still missing, and no matter how hard they tried, she could not be found. Lizzie looked at the calendar a few days later and decided that it was time to begin the journey.

Lizzie told Pearl, Branch and Dwarfer about her decision. They all agreed and wanted to do a test run of the file receiver before they started their journey. The others were on board with the idea right from the beginning and decided to meet once more at the Travelers Café to set up.

The very next day, the bunch went down to the basement of the café, so they could install their file receiver unnoticed. They copied the menu file of the café and sent it to the receiver. Fingers crossed, the tech group opened the device to check for the copy and to their delight, it worked perfectly. The groups congratulated each other, knowing that they were ready to begin.

Lizzie met one last time with Pearl, Dwarfer, and Branch at the inn. Damien had prepared a hearty tea of pastries, scones and jam, biscuits, and the tea itself. The tea reminded Lizzie of her mother when she made tea for a guest. Lizzie badly wanted to see Annie, her Mum and Dad, and the whole farm, but she needed to save Fantasia first.

Everyone enjoyed the food and chatted about their plans for after Sophie had been overthrown. Damien and Lizzie had planned a little treat for the team. Damien had tickets to the downtown fair, an awesome place filled with carnival games, rides, and food. They went on rides such as bumper cars and the waterlog, played games like hook the duck and balloon darts, and had a great time, but most importantly, they made memories.

Damien had brought a camera and he took photos of the group. On their way back to the inn, Damien quickly went to the print shop and printed the pictures. He showed them the pictures, and they had to admit it, they were awesome. Damien handed one picture to each person.

Lizzie looked at hers carefully. It was a picture of them riding the waterlog. They were drenched in water, laughing happily. Lizzie wondered if they would ever see each other again. She put the picture into her pocket as their cart train reached the inn. Lizzie and Damien said goodbye to Pearl, Dwarfer and Branch. They would be meeting the next day to depart, and they needed a good night's sleep.

The next morning Damien woke Lizzie and handed her a bag. The bag was filled with delicious goodies he had made. Lizzie thanked him gratefully at breakfast. They were supposed to pick up Pearl, Dwarfer, and Branch after lunch, so Damien played a round of Jacks with Lizzie, and for a short while, Lizzie felt like she was on the farm again, just playing and enjoying life. However, doing something important, something that would make life better felt satisfying, it felt like Lizzie was useful. Lizzie began feeling she was someone in the world, someone who was ready to make a change.

As time passed by, it was soon afternoon and they climbed onto the cart to pick up the others. First, they collected Branch, next they traveled to a hotel called the Homey Houses to pick up Pearl, and lastly, they walked over to the nearby Dwarf town to find Dwarfer and his cottage. After a while, they had finally reached the Café where dozens of people were waiting for them.

When they arrived, they were engulfed in a series of cheers and praises. Someone held up a banner that had the words "Down with the White Queen" written on it. The team edged their way through the crowd and into the café, where the others were waiting for them.

They congratulated each other on their hard work and wished good luck to Lizzie, Dwarfer, and Pearl. One group was going to attend the meeting of Just Soc that very day and show Alexa yet another one of their little tricks. Cooper, Lora, and their friends were staying in the basements of the Café, tracking, and checking the file receiver.

The basement room was full of people rushing around frantically, to make sure that everything started well. Branch was organizing a search party to find Flutter. Cooper and Lora were instructing their group on how to use their device. The device, called **"FileCopy"** was constructed using a series of complicated mechanism. It could be either a huge success or a miserable failure. However, Lora and her friends had a well- known company, which developed devices of all kinds, so they had the trust of a lot of people.

Pearl had decided that she and Lizzie would travel the same route, while Dwarfer would take another path. They all thought that they should bring Walkie-Talkies since they would need a way to communicate. It was better than sending letters or something since someone could read a letter and report them to the Queen.

After waiting around for an hour or so, Pearl told Lizzie and Dwarfer that it was time to leave. As they walked out of the room, they got a lot of thumbs-ups and hugs from each other. When they walked to the motorbikes they had prepared for the trip, they saw the crowd cheering for them, loud and proud. They had all the support. It was now up to them to bring justice to Fantasia. All three of them put on their helmets, mounted their bikes, and sped away into the distance.

They rode together for a while, until they came across a two-way road. Pearl and Lizzie needed to take the left to access their first portal, whilst Dwarfer had to go to his right. They quickly said goodbye and continued their paths.

Late in the evening after a long time on the road, Pearl and Lizzie came across a brightly lit town, where a seemingly large party was going on. Crowds of people danced on the streets to the loud music. Suddenly a tall man jumped out of nowhere and started speaking in such a fast tone that Pearl and Lizzie could not follow him. When the man saw the puzzled looks on their faces, he quickly switched to a slower, heavily accented English.

"I'm Rodrigues, and I am the mayor of this town. We are celebrating the birthday of my twins. They are turning 8 years old. Why don't you come to celebrate with us?" the tall man introduced himself.

Before Pearl could answer, Lizzie surprisingly agreed and motioned for her to come and join her on the dance floor. The people were friendly and excited, although they seemed quite bored of celebrating the mayor's children's birthday. Most people spoke good English, much easier to understand than Rodrigues's accented English. The two of them got to know a few other people around the town. When they got tired, they decided to head to the nearby motel. As they headed over, they encountered the twins.

"Hi! We're Diego and Lola! We are the children of the mayor. Are you the new people Papa was telling us about?" the twins asked.

"I am Pearl, and this is Lizzie, and we work for a company that does awesome explorations around Fantasia. We happened to come across your beautiful town, and we met the mayor. By the way, Happy Birthday!"

"Does your so-called company support the Queen?"

"Ugh! All our town hates her and anyone supporting her will be punished. By the way, I know that your company doesn't even exist. Just because I'm 8-year-old sweetie Lola, doesn't mean I don't know anything. I've got brains too, you know!"

Diego muttered something to Lola that Lizzie couldn't understand.

"No, we are on our way to the nearby portal. We are heading to the palace, on a mission to overthrow the Queen" Lizzie answered, ignoring Lola's side commentary.

"Woah! So, you are the guys who came up with Operation Justice?"

Sea and Lizzie were astonished by how far the news had come. "Well, not exactly, Diego. Lizzie here came up with the idea, and a few other friends including me helped Lizzie form the operation. News does spread fast around here!".

Diego was intrigued about everything that Pearl mentioned. He constantly asked mind-stumping questions so that Lizzie and Pearl had to think hard to answer. After a while, as they walked back to the party, Lizzie thought about Diego's interesting questions.

Diego seemed to be quite smart, but no one in this town had realized it. They seemed to be too focused on Lola, who was the prettiest girl around, sang like an angel, and danced as gracefully as a swan. Even today, on his birthday, no one had given Diego their wishes nor given him any presents. Lizzie was quite sure that no one would have noticed if he had disappeared.

An idea struck Lizzie's mind. With Diego's intelligence, they could find a better way of entering the palace, without being discovered. She was sure Diego would do anything to have such a great opportunity.

Lizzie searched around for Diego until she found him sitting alone by a park bench. She went and sat down next to him.

"Diego, how would you like to join us on our mission? Your talent could be very useful for us" Lizzie asked.

"Really? I...I would love to! When are we going to leave?"

"Tonight, I want you to meet me and Pearl at this same bench, with all your most important things. Bring dark clothing and be on time. I'll see you there" Lizzie said and walked back to Pearl.

Lizzie told Pearl about what had just happened. "Are you serious! You're bringing an eight-year-old on this dangerous mission?" Pearl raged.

"Don't worry, I'm sure that his knowledge will be very helpful for us at the palace. Nobody will notice his disappearance here anyway. Let us not underestimate his talents"

Pearl took a moment to think and eventually nodded. They continued to enjoy the party with the others until it was night. Surprisingly, the people had been partying all day, and they seemed to never stop. This was a perfect opportunity for Lizzie and Pearl to sneak out. They crept over to the park bench, quietly in the dark. Diego was already waiting; he had brought a large satchel with him. He waved excitedly as they approached him.

The three of them quietly walked over to their motorbikes. Pearl and Diego got onto one motorbike; Lizzie on the other. They all put on their helmets, turned on the engines, and sped away into the night.

THE FIRST PORTAL

The first portal was not so far away. Lizzie, Pearl, and Diego passed buildings and parks, shops, and trains. By the time they reached the portal, the sky was already pitch black. The stars sparkled, whilst the moon shone in its crescent shape. The portal glowed with a bright ray of light. One by one Lizzie and Pearl rode through the portal.

The moment they were in the portal seemed so magical. They were floating in a dimension covered in glitter and glamour. Creatures walked around looking beautiful as if they were models from Paris. Laughter and happiness seemed to overtake all the citizens. Where has this portal taken me? Lizzie wondered.

Diego seemed to be having the time of his life. He seemed cheerful and intrigued. In every little thing he saw, he cherished each moment of joy.

They rode their bikes into the town until they landed in a traffic jam. Loads of vehicles stood there, the drivers honking at one another. Behind Pearl, Lizzie, and Diego a car honked at them loudly. The driver sounded the horn again and again which irritated Pearl intensely. Pearl turned around and pointed at the traffic jam so that the driver could see. Even so, the driver still didn't stop.

Pearl parked her motorbike, lifted the glass shield of the helmet, and stomped over to the car behind them. She knocked on the window and motioned for the driver to lower the window.

"Hey, you stop honking at us. Can't you see that there is a traffic jam in front of us?" Pearl grumbled, annoyed.

"Hi Pearl, seeing each other after a long time, huh?" the driver said.

"Peony, Is that you? You've changed a lot!"

"Yes. It's me, Peony! You still look like the same old Pearl I knew since we joined Aquarius Academy. I just honked to get your attention. How's your mission going?"

"It's going alright. We've crossed the first portal, which brought us here. Anyway, where are we? I forgot the name of this place"

“You have come to Pixieville, home to more than a thousand different species of Pixie. My husband is from Pixieville, and I moved here since he can’t live underwater for that long. If you are planning to stay here for a while, you can always come and ring my bell. You are always welcome!” Peony exclaimed and drove away.

Pearl, Diego, and Lizzie decided to stay in Pixieville for the night. They had been traveling for long enough and definitely could use some rest. They ate dinner at a small restaurant and started looking for a place to stay. They remembered Peony’s invitation and headed over to the address she had mentioned earlier.

Lizzie rang the doorbell and almost immediately Peony opened the door with a warm welcome. She invited the three of them over to her couch which was comfortable. She laid a few biscuits and some tea out on the table and said, “It’s never the wrong time to have a cup of tea!” Lizzie sipped her tea and nibbled at her biscuit while listening to the conversation happening between Pearl and Peony.

After a while, Lizzie and Diego eventually got bored and asked if they could go to sleep. Peony led them into two different rooms on the top floor. Lizzie chose the first room and Diego the second. They both fell asleep immediately. After a while, Pearl and Peony decided to get a good night's sleep for the next exciting day as well.

The next morning, Peony and her husband prepared a delicious assortment of bread, cheeses, jams, cereals, juices, and milk. They hungrily munched it down and again started up some conversation between Peony's husband, Sap, and Pearl.

They were arguing about the best kind of jam. Pearl strongly believed that strawberry jam was the best of all, but Sap strongly disagreed. He believed that orange marmalade tasted divine. So, while their dramatic squabble went on, Lizzie and Diego crept upstairs to grab the Walkie-Talkie. They were planning to check in with Dwarfer. Lizzie turned it on and pressed the button to speak.

"Dwarfer, Lizzie speaking, can you hear me? over" Lizzie asked.

"Yes Lizzie, I can hear you. How far have you reached?"

"We've crossed the first portal, and we have picked up someone who could be useful for this mission. He is currently with me, but we should wait till we come to our common portal."

"Alright, I have also crossed my first portal and I am in Pixieville. I agree, a few more days and we will see each other at the common portal. Bye for now!"

"Who were you talking to again?" Diego curiously asked.

"That was just Dwarfer. Dwarfer, by the way, is also part of this operation. He's just taking a different route, so people don't become suspicious of us going together"

"Oh…I see. Interesting. Anyway, when do we have to leave?"

"I don't know, it depends on when Pearl wants to leave. I mean, we do have to get to the other portals on time"

They decided not to interrupt Pearl in her jolly mood. Lizzie showed Diego the maps they had made, routes they had marked, and the pictures they took. He was fascinated and interested to help. He kept asking for things he could do. Lizzie got irritated after a while of that.

"Hey Diego, can I ask you a favor?" Lizzie requested.

"Yes, of course, I am always ready to help," he nodded and spoke.

"Could you go downstairs, wait five minutes, and bring Pearl upstairs? Lizzie instructed.

"Can do!" Diego saluted and marched out of the room.

"What a silly little boy, but still so smart and kind!" Lizzie thought, giggling merrily.

Diego pulled up a chair to the table, next to Pearl. He watched how she laughed happily. She seemed to value her friendship with Peony. He sat alongside her listening to the conversation. After a while, he tapped Pearl's shoulder and pointed towards the stairs. He started walking over to the staircase, waiting for Pearl to come and join him. She eventually got up and ran upstairs cheerfully.

They pushed open the creaky door to reveal Lizzie drawing a map on paper with blue and black ink. She gestured for the others to come over to see her work. She had drawn a map of all the towns and forests, lakes, and oceans. It was a perfect replica of Fantasia. Pearl and Diego stared at the masterpiece in awe. Lizzie stood up and admired her work alongside the others.

"It indeed is a masterpiece, isn't it? It shall be one of my greatest memories to keep, it will remind me of my time here in Fantasia with all of you!" Lizzie admiringly declared. The two, still staring at the map, nodded in amazement.

"Why, you two believe that I drew this map?" Lizzie asked. They sheepishly nodded. "I was messing with you! I just put one of the maps we brought along with us and some inkwells in front of me and you guys fell for it!" Lizzie giggled. All three of them got a good laugh that morning because they knew that a day without laughter was a waste.

The day passed quickly at Peony's house. They ate lunch, played some checkers, had some tea at teatime, and before they knew it, it was time for them to leave. Lizzie, Diego, and Pearl carried their bags to the motorbikes. They said their last goodbyes, put on their helmets, and sped away into the distance.

Pixieville was quite a large town, so it took them a while to leave. By the time they had reached the edge of town, it was already midnight. They wanted to find a place to sleep, but all the fields they saw around them were filled with crops, and they were pretty sure that the land belonged to someone. Lizzie didn't mind about not getting enough sleep, but she was worried about Dwarfer.

Dwarfer had started smoothly, but in the end, he ended up with more problems than necessary. He had entered a place called Shapeshift Forest. When he first entered, he only saw a vast forest of trees, but during his sleep on the first night, he awoke in his tent to see a creature somewhat like Branch picking at his bag. When the creature saw that Dwarfer was awake, it quickly dropped everything it was holding and ran away. Now that Dwarfer didn't have a safe place to sleep, he knew that he needed to cross the second portal the next night.

He was about to set off, as the same creature he saw last night reappeared in front of him. "Hi, my name is Leafy. I am sorry for looking at your things last night. I didn't see you and I thought someone had left their bag here. We usually check what's inside everything, and we're almost always able to tell which tree it belongs to. But you're not a tree, so I wasn't able to tell who it belonged to. Then you woke up, and I got scared so I ran away. I just wanted you to know that I'm really sorry. Please don't leave because of me" Leafy apologized.

Dwarfer, relieved that he could trust this large area of forest, replied "It's alright, I get a bit nervous when I see strange and new things as well. Now I can cross this vast forest at my own pace. I won't be leaving for a few days or so anyway".

The two got along very well and Leafy guided Dwarfer through the trees, showed him the beautiful ponds, and introduced him to the large community. He found out about errors on his map and realized that the countryside he was crossing was larger than he thought. Dwarfer decided that he would enjoy his time with his new friends until it ended.

UNEXPECTED INVITATION

Lizzie, Diego, and Pearl had been traveling throughout the night and they were exhausted by the time dawn came. They came to a halt at a seemingly friendly ranch. Lizzie huffed and slouched on her motorbike, Pearl yawned loudly, and Diego stretched his arms out into the sky. "When are we ever going to stop somewhere? Diego and Lizzie both moaned.

"Stop whining you two, we will find a place at some point," Pearl said.

Suddenly, the door to the cabin on the ranch creaked open. A lady walked out over to them. "A few tired travelers, aren't you? You better come in and get some rest. Y 'all look like ragged old hags, but I think you aren't that old. The name is Bethilda. Hop on in!" the lady joked.

The three tired travelers walked into Bethilda's cabin. It was wonderfully lit with a small chandelier and the warmth of the fireplace was just so soothing. When Lizzie sat down on the couch, the cushions were so comforting and fluffy and the couch itself was of pure comfort.

They were served the warmest hot chocolate topped with marshmallows and whipped cream. “Divine!” Pearl remarked. Bethilda bowed in a funny way, which made Diego burst into laughter. She also made cheesy sandwiches, Diego’s favorite. They happily enjoyed all the delicious food that Bethilda had prepared.

Bethilda went outside to do some work on the fields. Lizzie, Pearl, and Diego all sat down on the couch. They spread out the different maps they had around the coffee table, including the one Lizzie and Pearl had drawn at the inn. They had made some progress on the map. The three had crossed the first portal and were quite near to the next. However, they couldn’t rest for long. They still had a mission to accomplish.

Lizzie, Pearl, and Diego all decided to help Bethilda out in the fields. As they approached her, Bethilda was harvesting wheat crops by hand and she looked quite tired. Bethilda finally noticed them and waved. The three pushed their way through the crops, all the way to where Bethilda was working. Diego picked up one of the sickles that lay near her and started to cut off the crops. All three of them, especially Bethilda, were surprised.

“Young man, where did you learn to do such good agricultural work? How old are you even?” Bethilda asked, surprised.

"I'm used to it. Mostly my Papa forgets about me because he is obsessed with my twin sister. For him, she is perfect. My Papa even wants her to become the next mayor after him! He owns a large field of crops, and he makes all the poorest boys come and take care of it. He sometimes forgets that I am his son and, so he sends me along with the other boys to harvest the crops".

"What a mayor! Such a disgrace! Does he work with the Queen?"

"Well, not really. I don't know. My Papa says that he is doing all he can to stop the Queen, but I don't know"

"I see. How did you end up with these two?"

"Well, they ended up finding our town on the day of my and my sister's birthday party and he invited them to stay for the party. He wanted as many people as possible to celebrate his perfect daughter, and just left me to be, even though it was also my party. Later on, Lizzie and Pearl found me and Lola, aka my sister, and Lizzie figured out that I was kind of bored there, so she decided to bring me with her and Pearl and now we are here"

Bethilda nodded. The two continued cutting off the crops as Lizzie and Pearl took a stroll nearby. Suddenly, a horse carriage stopped right in front of them and a tall man wearing a suit stepped out.

"Miss Shelly! There you are! You're invited to the Queen's special dinner at Rodney's tonight. Anyway, what are you doing with this old lady here? Oh! Princess Pearl! Is that you? I apologize for calling you an old lady. You are also invited to the special dinner tonight. See you there!" The messenger hurriedly handed the invitations.

He stepped into the carriage and as it slowly pulled away Lizzie and Pearl felt quite delighted. At the special dinner, they would be able to gather information about the Queen and her plans. They excitedly skipped down to Bethilda and Diego to tell them the good news.

When Bethilda heard the news, she asked "What's going to happen to Diego while y 'all are at dinner?"

Lizzie and Pearl looked at each other and wondered. "Just messing with you. I'll take care of Diego on the ranch while you're gone. I hope you got something to wear. I know y 'all are heading to the Queen's palace, aren't you? You'd better do some good work there. She will punish you hard for a single mistake, I'm sure you already know that. Hop along and get ready now!"

Pearl and Lizzie headed over to the cabin to get dressed for the evening. They had remembered to bring a few dresses just in case. Lizzie chose a long red silk dress while Pearl chose a turquoise gown with shimmering sequins. They each had a pair of matching heels and purses as well. Pearl led her long hair free. Lizzie undid her braids and let her curly hair bounce on her back freely.

"This will do!" she exclaimed.

Meanwhile, Diego had been helping Bethilda harvest crops from the field. She told him her funniest jokes, and he laughed at all of them

"Where does passion come from? A passion fruit!" they chuckled. As Lizzie and Pearl were about to enter their specially reserved carriage, they saw how Bethilda, and Diego laughed together cheerfully. They were sure that Diego was in safe hands. The carriage driver shouted, "Excuse me, please board the carriage, or else you'll be late!". They took one final look before getting in.

The carriage had red satin cushions, beautiful silk curtains, and a magnificent golden crown that sat on the very top. The windows were made from hard glass, whilst the carriage itself was crafted from gleaming birch wood. The scenery outside the window seemed so magical. It took them a while to reach Rodney's because it was far away from the ranch. At last, they were finally there. They opened the large doors to the restaurant and slipped in, not knowing what was in store.

A VERY FANCY DINNER

The Restaurant was crowded with people eating platters of food. Waiters in fancy black tuxedos walked around on their toes balancing large, full plates. Suddenly, a strange man approached them. "Names please!" he barked.

"I'm Princess Pearl and with me is my attendant Miss Shelley. May we please be let into the dining room?"

"Yes, this way please"

The stranger led them through a long room full of people seated at tables. They then walked up a tall staircase before they finally reached the door of the dining room. The door was covered in patterns, painted in shades of blue and white, colors of the Queen's liking. The man opened the door for Pearl and Lizzie. He bowed for them as they walked in. Just after them, a few other people walked in. They rudely threw their invitations at the man and walked away laughing.

Lizzie and Pearl stood nearby and had been watching the whole time. They carefully checked that no one was watching, and quickly rushed over to the poor man. "Are you alright sir?" they asked politely.

"I'm just fine, you needn't care about me"

"Of course, you do matter to us! Now tell us, does this happen every time there is a royal dinner?" Lizzie calmly questioned. He nodded.

"Does it bother you?" Pearl asked. He nodded again.

"Did you tell anyone that you are being treated like this?" they both queried. To their surprise, the man shook his head.

"Why not? Someone could have helped you!" they said.

"You wouldn't understand if I told you why. Now go, the Queen awaits you..." the man mysteriously said and slammed the door in their faces. Pearl and Lizzie hurried over to the table, found their table cards, and sat down at their assigned places. Luckily, Lizzie and Pearl were seated next to each other. However, the Queen was not so far from them, so they couldn't talk because they would be heard. Almost every spot was already filled.

They waited a few minutes for the last people to arrive. The last person who walked in wore a long, breezy white dress with intricate details. Her hair was as white as snow and was quite long. She had a golden tiara with a ruby similar to the one on Lizzie's amulet at the very top. Lizzie gasped. It was the White Queen.

She walked over to her seat and gently sat down. Queen Sophie had those bright blue eyes, which brought out her other features. But those eyes were also intimidating. They manipulated, cheated and hurt the world. Lizzie just wanted to see the look of defeat in those eyes.

"Welcome to dinner at Rodney's, brought to you by me. Today we are having our grand dinner, we will be discussing important kingdom matters and eating divine food. We also have some marvelous musicians present today, and to hear their music, you just need to snap twice, and they will start playing. Shall we begin with the appetizers?" Sophie welcomingly asked.

The people murmured as the tall waiters carrying the gourmet dishes placed the various appetizers on the table and guests oohed and aahed as more waiters kept coming in. After ten minutes of watching waiters bring in appetizers, they were finally allowed to start. Some, who were seated near Pearl and Lizzie ate hungrily, stuffing as much as they could in their mouths. However, Lizzie and Pearl themselves tried to look polite and took a little bit of everything. There were too many appetizers to count on the buffet table.

As the banquet went on, Lizzie discovered her favorites. Since the restaurant was based on foods from Earth, Lizzie quite enjoyed everything and went back for more of the delicious salad and traditional English dishes. The waiters kept bringing in more and more food. Some other favorites of Lizzie's were the French fries, the carefully crafted Sushi rolls, the delicious Italian pasta, the trés leches cake, the tiramisu, and finally the ooey-gooey cinnamon buns.

The cinnamon buns reminded her of the days she spent at Mrs. Browne's house. They were warm, cozy, and glazed and tasted exactly like how she made them. No matter how many of those buns Lizzie ate, she knew she could never forgive Mrs. Browne ever for what she had done. She had lied to Lizzie when she said that she was trustworthy.

It took everyone a while to finish eating before the discussions began. First, Queen Sophie talked about some boring fundraiser she wanted to start. That didn't interest Lizzie at all, so she asked to be excused to go to the bathroom. There she took out her Walkie-Talkie and pressed on the button. She was about to say hello as she heard footsteps outside the door. She quickly stashed it away and pretended to wash her hands.

It was the Queen. She gave a quick nod as if to say hello and walked into one of the stalls. Lizzie finished her "hand washing" and quickly walked back to her seat next to Pearl. Pearl looked at Lizzie questioningly, but Lizzie only shook her head in disappointment.

The Queen had re-entered the room and resumed her discussion about her fundraiser. Lizzie could see that a lot of the others were quite bored as well. However, they did nothing, for they knew Queen Sophie would punish them badly if they interrupted her.

At one point, the Queen started to talk about an interesting subject. She spoke about her throne.

"At some point, I need an heir to my throne, but I am not going to have an heir. I'm going to have a clone to take my place! I have the newest software to create clones. I've tested it, prepared it, and now, in just a few more days, I will be inviting all of you to watch the cloning of Queen Sophie!" she announced.

Lizzie felt sick. A clone of the White Queen? That would mean having to live for ages with another Queen just like Sophie. She knew they had to do something about it. In a few hours, they'd be back at the ranch with Bethilda and Diego. So, she patiently waited for Sophie to finish her conversations with the other guests. They talked about some important events, places, etc. that Lizzie had no clue about, so she didn't need to listen anyway.

Pearl felt exactly like Lizzie. She knew that a clone of Queen Sophie would be a problem. She still listened to the rest of the discussions because who knows what, there might have been some important information mentioned. At last, it was time to leave, and Lizzie and Pearl went outside of the dining room and back into the main hall. Before they were about to exit through the doors, they again met the strange man from earlier.

"Hello! Nice to see you again. What's your name?" Pearl kindly asked.

"I'm Antonio, from earlier today. I hope you succeed in your mission! The news reached the village. Hope you had a great time at Rodney's!" he said and left.

They were even more surprised how fast the news had traveled all the way to Rodney's. They quickly hopped into their carriage which would take them back to the ranch. Lizzie hoped that Diego hadn't been naughty while they were away. Moments later, the little carriage bounced onto the road back to the ranch.

By the time they returned, it was midnight and Diego had fallen asleep on the cozy little couch in the sitting room. Bethilda snored beside sleeping Diego. Pearl and Lizzie crept by quietly on their tippy-toes, making sure not to wake them up. There was a room with two freshly made beds and a bathroom that Bethilda and Diego had set up for them. They quickly got into their nightgowns and instantly fell asleep.

A HIDDEN SECRET

Dwarfer had left his fellow tree friends and was on the way to another portal. It was sad to say goodbye, but he knew it was for the best. It seemed like ages ago that he had seen Flutter "I wonder if Branch and the others have found Flutter yet" he thought.

But no one had talked about Flutter since the mission had begun. He decided to find out the truth himself. He turned on his Walkie-Talkie "Hello, Lizzie. Can you hear me?" Dwarfer asked.

"Yes Dwarfer, I can hear you just fine. What's your news?"

"Have you heard anything about Flutter? And when will you be at the second portal?"

"No, not yet. I think it will be a while by the time we do reach the next portal. How far are you?"

"Same as you. Any news from you guys?"

Lizzie immediately told Dwarfer about the Royal dinner. "Oh yes! We got invited to the Queen's Royal dinner at Rodney's, and we sort of overheard her discussion of cloning herself. She wants to clone herself so when she dies, her reign would continue. I will tell you in more detail the next time we meet. See you!"

Dwarfer was upset that their discussion about Flutter hadn't gone so well. Nobody seemed to care about finding her. He sighed and continued his journey to the next portal.

Whilst all of this was happening, the HQ was in absolute chaos. Alexa wouldn't accept the fact that Lizzie, Dwarfer, and Pearl wouldn't come to their meetings. "How are we ever going to begin our mission if nobody takes this seriously! I'm going to go hunt down those three and get them back to HQ, they'll see what happens when they keep missing meetings" Alexa announced angrily. The others quickly finished their work and left the HQ to go to their workspace, the basement of the Traveler's Café.

They decided to call Lizzie and Pearl. Lora, Cooper, and Branch sat together and turned on the Walkie-Talkie. "Hi! HQ speaking. Everything going well?" Lora whispered through the Walkie-Talkie.

"Yeah! All good. We are on track. About to reach the second portal. What about you guys in HQ? Everything going as planned? Is Branch there?"

"Yes, I'm here. Things aren't so good. Alexa won't buy our tricks, and now she is on the hunt for you three. You guys must make sure that you haven't left behind a single clue! And Flutter is still missing..." Branch reminded them.

"I'll tell the others about what you said. Dwarfer asked me about Flutter, but I didn't know anything either. Anyway, I need to leave right now, so talk to you later."

Lora, Cooper, and Branch looked at each other. Were Lizzie, Pearl, and Dwarfer going to be able to complete the mission in secret? Would Alexa find them? Would they be caught by the Queen and held hostage? They didn't know. They just had to hope for the best.

Lizzie and Pearl had woken up in the morning just as Diego and Bethilda appeared into the room with two full trays. They had a quick breakfast in bed, then stood up and got dressed for the day, and finally talked to Dwarfer and the HQ. Flutter was still missing, and nobody had paid attention to that. What if Flutter's disappearance had something to do with Queen Sophie wanting to clone herself?

A plan started to form in their minds. All they needed to do to solve the mystery of Flutter's disappearance was to get some help from Antonio, the man they had met yesterday in the Restaurant. They were sure he would help, for they had promised him that they would end the reign of the White Queen. He would probably have heard something about disappearing creatures whilst working in the palace.

They found Diego with Bethilda out on the fields. Since they needed Diego for this mission, Bethilda would have to spend the day alone. Diego was excited to come along for the mission. They said their quick goodbyes to Bethilda and walked over to the motorbikes. Lizzie, Pearl, and Diego put on their helmets and quickly got onto the motorbikes. They decided to go and check Rodney's, but they couldn't find Antonio there. Next, they went to the local stores, but the same thing happened. Then they checked the village, the park, the barns, and lastly the carnival, yet again and again he was still nowhere to be found. Suddenly Pearl remembered that she had forgotten to check at the waterfall of dreams. They followed her along the wide and narrow, short, and long roads across the town.

The waterfall of dreams was a mesmerizingly beautiful place. The rushing water glinted in different shades of rainbows when the strong sun shined. Plenty of families seemed to be having picnics just by the side of the pretty waterfall. Lizzie, Pearl, and Diego jumped off the motorbikes and started to scan around the place looking for Antonio. After a while of looking around, Diego spotted a tired-looking man sitting by the water while throwing little pebbles. That lonely figure was Antonio.

Lizzie, Pearl, and Diego hurriedly rushed through the picnic ground over to the place where Antonio sat. "Hi, Antonio! It's Miss Shelly and Princess Pearl from Rodney's last night. Don't you remember us?" Lizzie and Pearl greeted him.

"Yeah! I do! Who's the little boy here with you today?"

"This is just Diego, my nephew. He always likes to come along with Aunt Shelley!"

"Ah. Surprised to see y 'all!"

"So... Do you mind if we ask you something?" Pearl asked.

"Sure! Go ahead!"

"Have you heard anything about the Queen cloning herself? Think back to when you worked at the... um... palace! You could have possibly heard someone talking about it while cleaning." Lizzie hopefully questioned.

"Hmm... I'm thinking... Oh! Now I remember! It was a few weeks back..."

"Go on..."

"As I was saying, a few weeks back, when I was still working at the palace, I overheard a conversation between the Queen and one of her ambassadors. I was dusting just outside the library, which was where they both were. As usual, I wasn't paying much attention to what I heard. However, something that I heard caught my attention. I heard the Queen talking about an army, pixies and pixie dust too. I wrote down their conversation on a scroll. I always keep the scroll with me, because if I left it lying around somebody might take it and I could get into some serious trouble. Hold on, let me get it" Antonio said, pulling out a torn piece of a scroll.

"Well, that seems quite interesting. This is some useful information" Lizzie stated.

Antonio cleared his throat "Ahem. Ok, here it is! This is what they said"

Queen Sophie: Did you keep that pixie in her cell? She MUST not escape. I am most definitely NOT going back out there to find one of those pixies again.

Ambassador: Which one, your majesty? You have brought back plenty of them.

Queen Sophie: You very well know which one, Martha. Cell 101 in the dungeons.

Ambassador: Ah yes. That one. Still locked up in that cell. How are you planning to create a large full-size army to take over lands outside of Fantasia? No one has ever done it before…
Queen Sophie: I CAN DO ANYTHING!! I'm a proper ruler, and I can have an army if I want one. If nobody will freely join, then I'll just have to make them. As a final plan, we'll use those pixies to clone me, that way I'll have full control of the army… I'll gain more territory and become the most powerful ruler of all time… Bahahaha!!!
Ambassador: Um. A. Great. Plan. Your. Majesty. Happy to help. Oh, a quick question. What's the name of the pixie in cell 101? She keeps screaming at me to address her by her name, but I have no idea what it is. She is a psychopath of a pixie!
Queen Sophie: Ah, yes. Flutter. Flutter is the name. Now I must leave, and by six sharp today, those workers had better collect my pot of pixie dust, and I expect you to see to that, Martha. Goodbye.
"That's all I could remember. Now please, I would like to enjoy my day off in peace." Antonio yawned.

"Thank you so much Antonio, for your help. Enjoy your day off! Bye!" Pearl yelled as she ran back to her motorbike with Lizzie and Diego.

"Now that worked out great! We'd better tell HQ and Dwarfer that we've found out where Flutter is. Now we've got two missions. 1. rescue Flutter and 2. copy all the information from the Queen. They will all be so relieved that we finally found out where Flutter is" Lizzie hurriedly exclaimed

They hopped back onto the motorbikes and sped back to the ranch. Bethilda joyfully came over to them. She greeted Pearl and Lizzie with tight hugs. When she came to Diego, she lifted him into the air and twirled him around. Pearl and Lizzie looked at each other. It was no lie that Diego and Bethilda were made for each other.

They were supposed to leave today. Lizzie took a moment and made a hard decision. They would leave Diego with Bethilda. They knew that she would care for him and love him dearly.

"Diego, could you come here?" Lizzie called. Diego rushed over to her. "Now, I know that you have become very fond of Bethilda. Why is that so?" Lizzie questioned.

"Oh...well... umm... my mother died when I was little. She was the only one who paid attention to me. So, when she died, it was like I didn't exist to anyone, except for Lola, who was still very rude to me anyway, and my father who occasionally remembered that he had a son too. You see, when you guys went out to dinner, Bethilda paid so much attention to me, and we spent every moment together. She reminded me of my mother. That's why I like her "

"Oh well. Let me tell you something. How would you like it if you could stay with Bethilda?" Lizzie offered.

"Uhh... I would be happy, but I would love to help you and your team so that we can help the people of Fantasia. I talked this over with Bethilda as well. I hope you don't mind"

Lizzie just nodded and walked back to the cabin with Diego.

A COMPLICATED RESCUE

They had a few hours before they would leave the ranch. Bethilda's eyes were all puffy and teary from crying because she knew life wouldn't be the same without Diego. Meanwhile, Lizzie and Pearl were chatting on the Walkie-Talkies. Lizzie called HQ, whilst Pearl called Dwarfer.

As Lizzie told Lora, Cooper, and Branch the good news, the three of them jumped around in joy. After talking to Lizzie, they instantly rushed to the others to tell them the good news. The news spread quite fast. Everyone in town was excited to know that they would be able to find Flutter again.

Dwarfer was also quite excited about the good news, although he wasn't quite sure why everyone was celebrating. Flutter wasn't even rescued yet, and who knew if the information was even true. A fuming Pearl scolded "Of course it's true, kindness never lies! What's gotten into you?". And with that, she slammed the Walkie-Talkie on the table and stormed away.

At last, it was finally time for Lizzie, Pearl, and Diego to leave. Bethilda gave Diego plenty of hugs (and cookies) for the road. She knew they would miss each other a lot. After the final goodbyes and tears, Lizzie and Pearl got their motorbikes ready and sped away. Bethilda, who was once again tearing up, put a hand to her heart and said, "I will always remember those sweet children, God bless them and their brave hearts".

Lizzie, Pearl, and Diego were headed to a little village called Gnomestown. They would be meeting up with Dwarfer there and would plan the rescue of Flutter. Since she was in the palace dungeon, it would be quite hard to get down there and back without getting noticed. To be honest, it was almost impossible and quite dangerous to rescue Flutter. They could get caught, Pearl could be discovered as the Princess of the Sea, they could get stuck or take a wrong turn. But with a little bit of faith, they believed that it would be possible and somehow, they knew they would be able to do it. They were going to rescue Flutter.

Gnomestown was quite far away from Bethilda's ranch. It was much nearer to the valley, which meant they would be closer to their destination. Lizzie engaged the fastest gear and waved as she passed Pearl and Diego on the other motorbikes. "Want to race? I'm all up for it!" Pearl shouted from far behind.

“Of course! Catch me if you can! Lizzie shouted back.

Diego was not ready for all of that. You could tell by the scared look on his face that he wanted nothing to do with the race. But once everything started, he was filled with a sense of energy and enthusiasm. He spotted large piles of snow as they passed by and within a matter of five minutes, he had made a pile of snowballs. One by one he began to throw them at Lizzie and Pearl, who were too busy racing to pay attention to what he was doing. Lizzie spotted Diego when he threw the first snowball at her. However, on the contrary, when Diego wasn’t looking, Lizzie approached him with quite a large snowball. Lizzie then threw it immediately at Diego. Diego turned around to see Lizzie laughing uncontrollably after he had been hit with the snowball.

“Oh, so this is how you are going to play it? Then the snow war begins now!” Diego screamed.

By then, Pearl had seemed to have caught up with attention to what had been happening. She first made two equally sized snowballs. Then she quietly tiptoed over to Diego. Diego was luckily not paying attention to her, so she could easily throw the snowball at him. Whack! The snowball landed on Diego. Pearl ran away giggling so that Diego wouldn’t think it was her.

"Hey, why do I have to be the one to keep getting hit!" Diego yelled.

They spent some time in the snow, continuing the snowball fight they had started. The three of them were filled with joy and laughter. Until after a while, Lizzie noticed the time.

"Oh no! We're running late! We're supposed to meet Dwarfer in Gnomestown within half an hour. How are we ever going to make it there on time?"

"Don't panic! If we start now at full speed, we'll arrive on time! Now get ready because it's going to be a wild ride!" Pearl shouted through the snow that had just started to pour down.

The three of them jumped onto the motorbikes and took off at full speed. Other drivers passing by were astonished by how fast the three of them went. When the three of them passed by, you couldn't even see them properly. They were just speeding blurs in the distance. It had stopped snowing and surprisingly, the sun had come out. It shone brightly like a diamond and created a wonderful and pretty rainbow in the sky.

Before they knew it, they had reached Gnomestown. All the dwarves there were bustling and chatting around. All of them looked quite happy. Lizzie, Pearl, and Diego kept scanning the large crowds for Dwarfer, but so far, they hadn't found him.

Suddenly, they heard a whisper from the bushes behind them. What could that be? They all wondered. “Psst. Guys. I’m right here. Quickly slip inside so that no one sees you” Dwarfer cautiously whispered. The three of them followed Dwarfer’s instructions. Fortunately, he was right there in the bushes, hiding from everyone else.

“Why are you hiding?” Diego blurted.

“Shush. We don’t want people finding us. To be honest, I don’t want people finding me”

“I want to know what’s happening too, you know. Even Pearl does, right?” Lizzie interrupted.

“Oh, shut up Lizzie! What’s wrong with you all?” Pearl scolded.

Dwarfer, Lizzie, and Diego just shrugged.

“Now, Dwarfer, would you mind telling us what is going on?” Pearl asked.

“Sure. So, um... basically when I got here, people thought I was a famous idol, apparently, I resemble somebody well known, and so the paparazzi and pretty much the whole town started chasing me down. So, to cut a long story short, the whole place is looking for me right now”

“Well, that’s helpful”

However, Diego seemed to be amazed by Dwarfer's popularity. "How did you even convince everyone that you were famous? I mean can you act out Shakespeare's plays as well as he can? So far, how many paparazzi have you seen? Is it true that the whole town is after you? I have so many more questions for you!" Diego burst with his usual queries.

Lizzie and Pearl looked at Diego as if to say, "This is not the right time". Diego wasn't paying attention, and so he ignored them. Pearl and Lizzie rolled their eyes in boredom. Diego yet again asked questions, and this time Lizzie and Pearl indicated and hinted that he should have not asked questions and yet again they were ignored. Finally, Pearl and Lizzie got so irritated, that they screamed at him to stop.

"For god's sake, stop screaming. You'll give us away and the paparazzi will find me. For you, young man, it would be my pleasure to answer your questions, but not right now. Anyways, we're here to figure out how to rescue Flutter" Dwarfer shouted.

All of them stood silently. They knew he was right. "What are we waiting for? Let's start!"

The four of them crouched in the bushes and began to put some ideas together. They again drew another map, showing their route through the palace. They chose the dark, quiet hallways and the long, narrow staircases. Everybody had contributed something to the conversation, even Diego.

After a discussion that lasted around an hour, they had finally created a foolproof plan to rescue Flutter. The palace was like a maze, but luckily Pearl had enough knowledge of the layout to be able to create a rough map of its structure. The team carefully examined the plan. It seemed impossible, but together they could complete the rescue successfully.

"Now this is what I would call a complicated rescue" Lizzie commented.

AT LAST, THE PALACE

Since almost all of Gnomestown was still searching for "the famous dwarf", the four of them quietly snuck out of the bushes and ran to hide. Luckily for them, no one had noticed their motorbikes. This town was not the safest place to stay. Before they knew it, the team had raced out of Gnomestown while the locals were still in their search troops, looking for their idol.

Lizzie, Pearl, Dwarfer, and Diego traveled together and all four of them easily crossed the second portal. They arrived in a dark, gloomy town. The skies were a pale shade of grey, and the trees were dry and droopy. The place seemed quite empty and lifeless, which gave it a spooky vibe. Lizzie noticed almost immediately that Diego seemed quite scared and uncomfortable around the unknown place. His teeth were chattering, and he was shuddering.

"Diego, are you alright there?" Lizzie yelled across the street. He nodded timidly. She motioned to Pearl and Dwarfer to continue ahead without stopping. The three motorbikes lurched forward into the darkness. It only took them a few minutes or so to pass through the frightening place and soon they had entered a bright and friendly-looking town, close to the valley of the palace. Lots of climbers headed to the great mountains. It was a tradition to climb up the valley, and then to take a picture near the palace.

The Queen usually didn't mind all the tourists. She was delighted, believing that more tourists around meant more publicity and more people would support her views. Tourists were part of her plan to rule all other lands including Fantasia. She was the only one that knew this, but the plan was stored in the secret files that she kept on her computer. Sophie stored all her private plans and information in those files, so they needed to be protected well. She had locked the room in which her information was stored. She had even put a password on all the computers and files. She was sure her information would be completely safe.

Lizzie, Pearl, Diego, and Dwarfer noticed that the town seemed unusually colorful. The trees were in different shades of blue, the clouds in the sky seemed to be different yellows, and the skies themselves had changed into a pattern of different hues of red. Every other thing in this unusual town was either red, blue, or yellow, except for the creatures, humans and animals. "What a strange place! I have the feeling we shouldn't be here for long" Diego said, unsure.

"Oh, it's just fine. We'll take our time" Dwarfer chuckled, although he was not so sure himself. The four of them sped through the crowds of people at the markets, passing by tall buildings and houses. In a matter of five minutes, they had already zoomed out of the strange valley. The valley of the palace was so close that they could hear all the climbers getting ready for an expedition.

"Hello there, mates! Here to climb?" one of the climbers asked.

"Oh no, we're not climbers. We're just here to enjoy the beautiful view and perhaps we might even use the cable car to go and see the palace" Pearl flatly answered.

"Oh well, then you must join us! Why don't you get some gear from the rentals?"

"But we aren't here to climb. We don't have time to climb. Plus, Diego here isn't old or tall enough to join in"

"Well then two of you can join us and one of you can go with Diego on the cable car" another climber interrupted.

"There we go, now that's a solution" the first climber triumphantly said.

Instantly, Pearl volunteered to use the cable car with Diego. She grabbed his hand and scurried up to the long line with Diego.

"Great, now we've got to go climbing while Pearl and Diego get to go on the cable car and not get tired at all" Lizzie moaned.

"Well, we're both in the same boat, so quit moping" Dwarfer snapped.

"Alright, alright. But seriously, it isn't fair that we must climb instead of using the cable car"

"Are you guys ever going to get the gear?" a climber yelled.

Lizzie and Dwarfer quickly ran and rented two sets of climbing gear. By the time they got back, the other climbers had already begun to climb. Lizzie and Dwarfer quickly caught up with them. They were able to take the lead, and as they reached the top Lizzie rang the enormous bronze bell. Pearl and Diego had been watching the whole time cheering them on to the top. They quickly jumped off the cable car and rushed over to help Dwarfer and Lizzie.

"How was the climb? Did you guys have any fun? I bet that y'all had so much fun that even I would care to join you!" Pearl teased.

"Not funny!" Lizzie mumbled under her breath. Dwarfer knowingly agreed.

"I'm just messing with you! Now c'mon, let's head over to the palace!"

The climbers led the four of them on a gravelly path lined with smooth, shiny pebbles. They walked on for a short time until they could see a little troupe stationed in front of the palace doors in the distance.

"We're almost there!" the climbers exclaimed.

Most of them stared at the structure, which was truly magnificent. Lizzie marveled over the beautifully crafted colorful glass panes. The palace itself was covered in patterns of all kinds. Zigzags, waves, polka dots, spirals. You could find just about any pattern.

Lizzie's eyes wandered over to the back of the palace. She saw neat rows of fruit-bearing plants, bushes, shrubs, veggies with long leaves, and tall, magical trees with exposed roots. A set of swings and a slide was placed nearby, with a wooden bench close by. However, everything was rotten, and the plants appeared to have dried up. Lizzie wondered about the state of the mysterious gardens.

"An amazing place, huh?" Pearl asked. Lizzie nodded, still staring at the gardens in front of her.

"My dear, I will tell you a tale that will solve many mysteries, bring truth to the world, and leave you to wonder. Shall I begin?" Pearl explained. Lizzie again nodded, not knowing what she was about to hear.

THE KING'S PALACE

On a long, sunny day before Queen Sophie was born, the King, her father, decided to build a palace. The King spent his leisure time drawing the most exquisite structures, and he decided that the palace would be his absolute masterpiece. According to the legend, he spent almost a whole year creating the masterpiece. The King spent every spare minute planning, creating, thinking, and implementing his ideas for the palace. His citizens anxiously waited, until he, at last, revealed the final design for his masterpiece. It was indeed magnificent. All citizens marveled over the precise patterns, the colorful glass windowpanes, and most of all, the gorgeous gardens. The gardens were filled with the most exotic plants, delicious fruit, and vegetables, and most importantly, joy. The King, after the gardens had been prepared, seemed happier than ever. He tried to spend all his time there. However, as days passed by, the joy of the time he spent in the gardens started to wear off. He then realized that pure emotion could never last forever. The King experienced the same after Queen Sophie had turned 16. He knew that he soon would have to pass on the kingdom of Fantasia to his daughter. The excitement he had experienced disappeared, and he soon changed his mind about ending his reign, and that decision led to his death.

* * *

Lizzie's curiosity increased by the second. As they formed a line to cross the drawbridge, Lizzie was still thinking about the story. There was something about it that triggered a memory. Something about that story seemed familiar.

THE CLIMBER CONVENTION

The soldiers yelled, “Hand over those tickets, you lousy twits!”. Instantly, tickets started piling up on the desk, and those who had forgotten theirs scurried away quickly. Pearl, Lizzie, Diego, and Dwarfer were tense. They had not brought tickets! However, one of the climbers quickly handed them four slips of paper and whispered, “Keep 'em safe, coz you won’t be getting new ones”. They placed their tickets on the pile in the front and slipped in through the wide doors of the palace.

The palace was specially decorated for the occasion. The group with tickets was led into a large ballroom filled with chairs and a single podium at the front. Many began to find themselves seats, so Lizzie motioned for them to find seats as well. They decided to sit at the back, so they could easily sneak out to rescue Flutter. Pearl luckily had already prepared and disguised herself so that she wouldn’t be discovered as the Princess of the Mermaids.

Earlier in Gnomestown, they had heard that the climber's convention would be starting in a few days at the palace. The four of them had decided that it would be the perfect opportunity to sneak into the palace and rescue Flutter. With the five of them, they would be able to easily distract the convention and sneak into the Queen's computer room.

The ballroom in which they were all seated was loud and noisy. The climbers were goofing around and messed up several rows of chairs while breakdancing. Many people gave them annoyed looks as they passed by, letting the climbers know that it wasn't amusing. The climbers still ignored everyone and continued to breakdance through the rows. Suddenly, all of them stopped dancing and instantly hopped onto chairs. The doors of the ballroom creaked open, and in came a tall, slender woman with shiny, silky blonde hair that seemed almost white, greeting and waving to everyone with a posh, ladylike accent and manner.

Lizzie recognized her as Queen Sophie. She did have snowy, pale skin and dressed in the most exquisite luxurious clothes. She didn't strike Lizzie as "dangerous" or "cruel" in the way she looked, but she understood how everyone feared to speak out against her because they all knew that she had the intention and the power to stop and harm them. Lizzie wasn't afraid. She would bring justice to those who deserved it.

Queen Sophie strutted over to the podium. In the same fashion, the speakers strutted over to the podium and stood behind Queen Sophie. She began, “Hello, dear citizens, today as you all know we are gathered for the climber’s convention. Climbing is a very important tradition here in Fantasia, and for the next few days, we will all gather here to appreciate that together. Here I have invited some of the most incredible climbers from across Fantasia to speak about their adventures in the wild. Let’s welcome them all to my palace!!”

One of the speakers stepped forward to the Podium. She was a tall skinny girl, looking about the age of 15. Her shrill voice boomed “Silence! I appreciate you all coming here to listen to me, and of course all the other speakers here today. I am Sonya Nobleheart, wild climber, daughter of Alexa Nobleheart, leader of Fantasia’s investigative force. Today I have prepared for you a talk about the qualities of a climber. To be a successful climber, one must have the divine characteristics of a good human”.

"I will now hand over to our next speaker, Algae Blue, a sea cave climber, and explorer, to explain to us about his talk and he will hand over to the next and so on until everyone has been introduced. Then there will be a brief intermission, where you all will have access to a grand buffet in the dining quarters. Soon after we will begin with the speeches, and there will be a few brief intermissions to follow. Algae, please come up to the podium" Sonya finished.

Lizzie, Pearl and Dwarfer couldn't believe it. Alexa was a traitor! Dan had been right. She immediately shut down Lizzie's idea because the Queen would be destroyed. Lizzie felt hot anger boiling inside her, Pearl was red with rage, and Dwarfer muttered rudely under his breath. Diego, however, had not the slightest clue as to why the three of them were in such rage and continued to listen to the speaker up at the podium.

They were planning to run off from the buffet. They wouldn't come back for the speeches. Instead, they would go to the dungeons, rescue Flutter, leave the palace from the nearest exit and then go away to a camping ground. "It's a solid plan" Lizzie had said earlier in Gnomestown.

They waited impatiently as all the speakers introduced themselves. As they finally reached the last one, one hour had already passed in the palace. "Attention please, now we will have a brief intermission so that our guests may eat food from the buffet. The dining quarters are one hallway away. For assistance, please ask one of our guides" Queen Sophie announced.

Immediately the four of them scrambled out of their seats and rushed out of the door in search of the dining quarters. They calmly walked through the long hallway from the ballroom and then saw two rooms, one to their left and one to their right. Diego checked the labels on each door. The one on the left was labeled "Cleaning Storage" and the one on the right was labeled "Dining Quarters". "I found the quarters! The room on the right is the dining quarters!" he cheered.

They pulled open the door and entered the room. Already lots of people had found their way in and started eating. Lizzie and Pearl merged with people at one corner whilst Diego and Dwarfer were in the other corner. According to their plan, they would stay in the dining quarters for a few minutes and then creep out and run down to the dungeons to find Flutter.

To pass the time while they waited, Dwarfer loaded his plate full of food. Diego unsurely watched as Dwarfer one by one stuffed things from the buffet in his mouth. Spring rolls, Sushi, Samosas, Schnitzel, Pumpkin pie, Muffins, Cupcakes, and a bit of everything else. Pearl noticed Dwarfer stuffing food into his mouth. She shook her head. He was just going to slow them down. However, she didn't know that Dwarfer was being extreme just to distract the crowd in the dining quarters.

One by one naturally people started to gather around the corner where Dwarfer stood. Diego had moved over to Lizzie and Pearl earlier, so they could leave the buffet. Gradually, all the crowd were watching Dwarfer eating like a monster. Dwarfer mouthed at them to leave. "Go on, I'll be there eventually". Pearl, Lizzie, and Diego crept out through one of the side doors and began the search for the Dungeon…

THE DUNGEONS

The three of them came across a three-way intersection. Pearl pulled out their map of the palace. She knew her knowledge of the palace would come in handy one day! "This way!" Pearl whisper-shouted while pointing straight ahead. They tiptoed like mice and whispered in such a whisper that one could barely hear, to make sure that not a single person, whether it was a servant, a guest, or the Queen herself would hear them.

Pearl directed them through the long hallways of what seemed like a maze. At last, after a long time of wandering, they reached a tall door followed by a staircase which descended into a deep, dark place, also known as the dungeons. "We're here. We've now got to enter the dungeon in the darkness" Lizzie whispered. The others nodded and followed Lizzie into what seemed to be a secret, tortured world.

The staircase in front of them was old and dusty, normal for a dungeon. The banisters were made of rusty metal, and the steps were covered in endless stains and scratches. Not a single light was burning, and even the windows were covered in black sheets behind many metal bars. At some point, a cold gust of wind entered through a small space in the window, making Lizzie, Pearl, and Diego shiver.

Lizzie stared at the window whilst walking and bumped into a set of metal bars. Pearl rushed over to Lizzie and muttered something about silly distractions. Meanwhile, Diego had forgotten about the mission and was wandering around examining the metal bars Lizzie had bumped into. There was a rusty metal plate with "Cell 101" engraved into it. Diego recalled something from the days before. He remembered that Antonio had mentioned something about a pixie called Flutter in cell 101. Flutter was a pixie, and she was somewhere here in the Dungeon. "Maybe cell 101 is the place to look" Diego wondered.

Diego crept over to Pearl, who was busy trying to awaken Lizzie by splashing water all over Lizzie's face. "That's not going to work. She hit her head a bit hard, so she'll be unconscious for a while" he explained. Pearl nodded.

"Anyway, before we go anywhere, I found cell 101. Lizzie bumped her head on that very cell. I suggest that we carry Lizzie while we investigate the cell"

"Well, we've gotta get out of here at some point, with Flutter, of course, so we might as well do what we can to find Flutter while Lizzie is knocked out. Let's go!" Pearl agreed approvingly.

The two of them heaved Lizzie onto their backs. Diego tried to open the cell by using the doorknob on the metal bars, but it wouldn't budge. He kept on pulling and pulling with all his strength, but it still wouldn't budge.

"Oh, silly goose! It's a dungeon, and they're not going to leave a cell door open for you just like that. Here, use this" Pearl giggled, pulling out a hairpin from her long, wavy hair. Diego carefully stuck the pin into the keyhole and twisted it. To his surprise, it worked, and they entered the cramped cell.

Cell 101 was empty except for a shard of glass from a bottle. They gently laid Lizzie on the ground and began to look for clues. Diego examined the brick walls, but he didn't notice anything. Annoyed, Diego slumped onto the wall and stumbled. A loose brick had fallen out, creating a large peephole. Diego immediately showed Pearl what he had found.

They looked through the hole and saw a bright beam of magical light. It sparkled and glittered, glimmered and shone. "Pixie dust" Pearl whispered in awe. A familiar face with a green pixie cut turned around to look.

"Flutter! You're here! We've been looking for you for weeks!"

"H…h…how did you guys f…f…find me?" Flutter stammered in fright, staring through the hole.

"We have our ways…" Diego slyly answered.

"Wh…wh…who is that boy?"

"Oh, this is Diego. Me and Lizzie found him on the way here. Long story short, we're here for a mission and we need you. I'll tell you everything later. C'mon, let's go!"

"B…b…but I'm stuck here" Flutter mentioned, showing the silver cuffs linked to chains on the wall.

"I think that if Pearl used her hairpin trick again, she'd be able to free you. I mean, there is a little keyhole for a key in each cuff" Diego suggested.

"Wait. I'll need to put the cuffs through the hole, so that Pearl can free me, and then I'll open the secret door. I've seen the people who came down here open it so many times, that I memorized their exact actions to open it. Ok, here. Unlock the cuffs"

"I suppose we could give it a try" Pearl agreed and almost immediately got out her hairpin and began to fiddle with the cuffs. She was fully concentrating on the lock, as Lizzie suddenly woke up.

"Um...Anybody? Hello! Why am I in this creepy place? Is this a dungeon? Please let me out if I am imprisoned for doing something terrible that I didn't do" she questioned fearfully.

"Ooookay. What's up with Lizzie?"

"Lizzie was staring at who-knows-what and bumped into the bars leading into your jail cell. Then she became unconscious and me and Diego carried her into your cell. Diego, go help Lizzie. Hold still, I almost got the first cuff" Pearl explained while attempting to free Flutter from the cuffs.

Diego kneeled next to Lizzie. She had seemed to have completely forgotten about their mission in the dungeon. He decided to take it easy since he knew that after having a slight concussion a person might be a little forgetful.

"Hi, Lizzie! I'm Diego. Do you remember me from the party?" he asked, looking back at what had happened in the past few days.

"Oh yes! You're the birthday boy with the twin sister! Where's Pearl?" Lizzie recalled. Luckily Lizzie only had a minor concussion, so she was able to recall everything that happened a few days ago.

Just about then, a cuff fell to the floor, and Pearl rejoiced. "I did it! I've unlocked the cuff! Now Flutter, I know that the amount of pixie dust you have right now is enough to break the other cuff. Hurry!" she celebrated.

Flutter muttered a spell and sprinkled her pixie dust over the cuff. Kaboom! The cuff had split into two and Flutter was now free. She quickly unlocked the door to the secret room and ran out to join the others. Lizzie, Pearl, Diego and Flutter had planned to escape, but they couldn't leave without Dwarfer.

Pearl suddenly remembered what Dwarfer had said. He had told them to leave and continue without him, and he would join them again at some point.

"Guys, remember what Dwarfer said earlier in the dining hall. We should leave without him because we know we won't find him if we try. He told us exactly that and so I think we should follow what he said. So, I am leaving now and if you want to you can join me and we will leave the palace and continue with our mission. If not, then you can search for Dwarfer and find out that he didn't ask us to do so" Pearl announced. The rest of them stood there silently taking in what they had just heard.

Surprisingly Flutter was the first one to come to her senses. “I’m going to join Pearl even though I don’t know what Dwarfer said and haven’t heard much about the outside world over the past weeks because I believe that Pearl is telling the truth and so is Dwarfer. They are my friends and so I will always stand with them not against” Flutter stated and stepped to Pearl’s right.

Slowly one by one, Lizzie and Diego agreed and stepped next to Pearl. They all tiptoed to the staircase of the dungeon. Diego slowly pulled open the creaky door and checked to see if the coast was clear. He silently nodded and Pearl led them out into the dark hallway. Not a single person was there and so they crept carefully through all the way long.

Pearl directed them through each and every hallway on her map. They took lefts and rights and went forward and backward until they reached the back door. They had decided that the drawbridge door would have been too obvious, so they decided to use the back door, which would lead them into the garden where no one was to be seen. There, they could easily jump over the fence and take the cable car back down to the valley. Diego once again checked to see if the coast was clear. He nodded, and everyone followed him out into the gardens.

The garden was indeed a dry, dusty place. The plants seemed to have not been watered for years, making them look lifeless. "Gee, the Queen really hates this garden. I mean, look at it, she doesn't seem like she wants to take care of it!" Diego mentioned in a loud whisper.

"Shh, you're going to get us caught" Pearl crossly whispered back.

"It's ok Pearl, no one is there to see or hear us anyways," a voice said out of nowhere.

"Dwarfer! You're here! I haven't seen you in so long!" Flutter immediately recognized.

"It's good to see you too, Flutter, but we must hurry now, because we're on a mission"

The four of them, now five, walked quietly around the garden, looking for the fence gate.

"There surely won't be any obstacles at the gate," Lizzie thought. However, she was wrong...

GATES AND GRAPEVINES

They had at last found the rusty, metal gates, but to their surprise, it had been covered in grapevines! They were long, dry, and lifeless grapevines. The gates were covered all the way with vines, making it almost impossible to jump over the gates, let alone climbing them.

"How in the world did this even get here?" Pearl wondered.

"How on earth are we going to get over this thing?" Dwarfer thought.

However, Flutter did something unexpected. She pulled out a little drawstring bag and poured some kind of sparkly shiny dust into her hands. The rest of them stood there watching curiously.

Next, Flutter sprinkled the dust all over the grapevine-covered gates. By that time, Lizzie, Pearl and Diego had figured out that it was her special pixie dust.

"What're you even doing with that? Like, do you think that dust is going to clear away those vines?" Dwarfer sneered.

"Shh, she's concentrating. By the way, that is pixie dust, and it was able to literally break a metal cuff link" Lizzie shushed.

"Pfft. Whatever, I still don't believe you"

They continued watching Flutter as she continued sprinkling pixie dust over the gates. Then there was magic. The Vines slowly transformed into wonderful shades of green. They began to rise from their drooping position, one by one. Then the grapes started to grow and become juicier by the second. The vines unwrapped themselves from the gates and slithered away.

Dwarfer and the others stared in awe. They couldn't believe what they had just seen. "Now do you believe me?" Lizzie asked him. He nodded. Flutter was just untangling the last vines from the gate as they walked over to her. "That was Great! Awesome" they high-fived and congratulated as they passed by.

They all walked out of the gates together, and Flutter used her magical pixie dust and somehow made the now lush green vines turn back to their pale, faded color and slip back into their place on the gates.

"That should do. Nobody will know that we left the palace from here!" she said, relieved.

They had done it. They had accomplished a complicated rescue. They were ready to execute their real mission.

They now needed to walk all the way around the palace, so they could reach the cable car without being noticed. They trudged along in the boiling heat. It would have been easier if they had left from the front door, but again, they would most likely have got caught.

After what felt like an hour, they had finally been able to walk the long way to the cable car. Not wanting to look suspicious, they ended up going in pairs. Lizzie and Diego hopped onto the first carriage together, with Dwarfer and Flutter in the one after. Pearl had decided to go alone because someone might suspect her if she went with one of the others, her being a princess.

Everyone gazed out of the windows to see the most beautiful view of the tall mountains as they descended into the valley. There were plenty of people in line for the cable car since the Climber's Convention was happening that week. Some people even brought tents with them so they could easily get a spot in the seats for the second round of the convention. "These people really want to go see the convention," Lizzie remarked.

Dwarfer had booked them 1 large and 1 small cabin for the night in the valley. They were planning to execute their mission plan tomorrow, when almost everyone would be at the convention. That way there was a lesser chance they'd be discovered.

They rode the motorbikes to the cabins they had booked. The girls took the large one while the boys went over to the smaller cabin. As the girls were getting ready for bed, Flutter asked a question that stumped them.

"Pearl, Lizzie, do you know how we're ever going to sneak in five people without having tickets to the convention?" she asked.

She was right. They had forgotten about sneaking back in the next day, and they knew they couldn't rely on the climbers this time.

"Hmm...Good thinking Flutter. Do you have any ideas?" Pearl doubtfully asked.

"Well, no, not at the moment. Oh, and I wanted to tell you, I won't be able to sneak in with you guys because if you get caught being with me while I'm supposed to be in dungeon 101, we'll all be in more trouble than necessary." Flutter reluctantly replied.

"You know Flutter, you're right. We can't have everyone going on the mission. We need people for other jobs, such as stalling, or even keeping track of all communication lines. I think we should call the others over and discuss the agenda" Lizzie agreed.

Pearl, after a moment's hesitation, agreed with them and immediately set to work. "Lizzie, go find out which channel the boys are on and tell them to come over immediately. Flutter, get a space for discussion ready. Make sure to get snacks, especially for Dwarfer. I'll get some other things for our little gathering ready. Hurry up, we haven't got much time!" Pearl instructed.

They all went about to do their share of the work. Lizzie had almost immediately found the correct channel and spoke to Diego and Dwarfer about the situation. They had said they would be there ASAP, and they did keep to their promise.

They were all gathered around a warm little campfire, which Flutter had easily conjured using her magical skills. Diego brought a large packet of jumbo marshmallows to roast on the fire while they discussed the agenda.

"WOW!! Marshmallows! How did you get them if you were with us the whole time? I didn't take you to any shop" a hyper Dwarfer asked excitedly.

"Well, long story short, I stole marshmallows from the fields when I worked at my family ranch" Diego explained.

"WAIT, you have a field full of MARSHMALLOWS in your ranch!!"

"Yup. There are lollipops, chocolate, gummy and licorice grain fields in the ranch. It's delicious"

"That is awesome, but we need to get to work. You can roast and eat your marshmallows while we talk" Pearl interrupted, annoyed by the irrelevant chat.

"So, Flutter asked a thoughtful question earlier, which led to this meeting. Flutter, please share your question with us. Go ahead!" Lizzie said, nibbling on a golden-brown marshmallow that she had just finished roasting.

"So, what I asked was if you guys already planned how we're ever going to sneak in five people without having tickets to the convention? You were lucky last time, but who knows what!" Flutter recalled.

"You know, she is quite right. I mean, we can't just walk up to the soldiers and say that we're there to spy on the Queen. We're going to get into big trouble by doing that"

The rest of them seemed to understand what Flutter had asked. They all immediately started to squabble about whose idea was the best, getting louder and louder until...

PREPARING FOR MISSION

"Ahhhh! There's a snake on my head! It's going to eat me up! Help!" shrieked a frightened Lizzie.

"It's alright, Lizzie, calm down. It's just a harmless Garter Snake. It won't bite you or anything. Watch!" Diego told her. He slowly led the small, green snake onto his arm. The Garter Snake inched its way up onto Diego's arm, which he had stretched out so that the little creature could easily climb up.

The others watched, mesmerized by the fact that the snake hadn't harmed Diego in any way. Soon they relaxed and even let the snake slither over to them.

"What a shock! But anyway, how did this snake even get into the cabin? We locked it up, closed the windows, pulled down the blinds, and yet a snake still gets in?" Pearl wondered.

"Yeah... about that. I know that none of us would let a Garter Snake into the cabin. So, you know, that snake is wild, aaaaannd... I'll tell you the rest later" Diego said, hurrying out to the door, grasping the Garter Snake by its head. The snake was gasping for air, squirming in the tight grip of Diego's hand. They all gaped at Diego.

"Diego! You are murdering that poor being! Just let him out into the wild!" Flutter shrieked crossly.

"I said, I'll tell you the rest, LATER! Just let me get this over with!" He angrily replied. They looked at each other. Why was Diego behaving so strangely? Diego stood near the door for the next five minutes, strangling the seemingly innocent snake to death. Once the snake had stopped breathing, Diego simply just tossed the dead thing out into the woods and slammed the door.

"Okay, now should I tell you why I did THAT?"

The four of them nodded silently. "That snake wasn't just any Garter Snake. It was a secret spy device. They can easily sneak in everywhere, even in places that are completely closed and locked. I recognized it at once because that would have been the only creature that could get into our closed cabin" He began.

"Why is this so-called 'Spy Snake' so dangerous?" asked Dwarfer.

"It records whatever we say, which means we would get into big trouble if the spy agencies knew what we're up to. That's why I immediately squashed it so that the recording chip would break. Now is it clear?" Diego answered.

“To be fair, I’m quite impressed by you and what you know. I didn't even know that! At first, I was concerned about having an 8-year-old on the team, but in the end, it doesn’t seem so bad. Good work, Junior” Pearl said, seeming quite impressed by Diego.

The rest of the team applauded Diego for his good work before they got back to their planning. This time, they decided to take it slowly so they would be able to plan it out. One by one, they shared their ideas within their little group circle and before they knew it, they had a plan.

They were to sneak back after lunch, because they’d then have a solid three hours to get everything done. Firstly, Flutter would use her pixie dust to let them in through the garden door, which Pearl said was always open. Then, they would follow their map to the computer room of the palace to access the information. Lastly, they would then transfer the data and everything through data transmitters to the team back at HQ, The Travelers Café.

They couldn’t bring everyone in, of course. Flutter had already pulled herself out because she would get into much more trouble than the others if she were caught. Dwarfer said he’d hang around with Flutter in Valley Town while the others snuck around in the palace to complete the mission.

Flutter spent the rest of the meeting making pixie dust and listening in at the same time. She made a big effort to have enough dust ready for the next day since pixie dust took time to process and they desperately needed it.

"So, list of things to do before we leave tomorrow, call HQ, pack resources and get some good rest. See you at 8 am SHARP!" Pearl said cheerfully, shoving the boys out the door to leave because it was already late into the night.

They got ready for bed in a jiffy, it was important to sleep to be awake and energized the next day. They all set alarms for the morning, so they wouldn't oversleep. The next morning was filled with beautiful, bright sunshine, so bright that they could all tell that the day was going to be a success.

Soon enough, they all met up at the large cabin at 8 am sharp, just as Pearl had said. The five of them ate a small breakfast of doughnuts and fruit salads from the store. "Boy, do I miss those big breakfasts at the inn!" Dwarfer said sadly. The others agreed. No one was a better chef than Damien.

Right after breakfast, all of them immediately jumped into the tasks that they needed to complete before leaving. They called HQ and told them about the mission plan, they packed, and they revised the mission plan again and again until they could fluently recite the whole thing.

At last, at noon they were finally done with their work, and they had a quick lunch of salad and toast. They were ready to leave for the palace Lizzie, Pearl and Diego marched out of the cabin with their knapsacks, Flutter and Dwarfer trailing behind them.

They walked all the way to the valley, then they lined up for the cable car. Once again, they went up each in different carriages, so they wouldn't be suspicious for even a second, even though half of Fantasia already knew what was happening. They couldn't risk being caught. After they all had reached the top, they slowly walked over to the back of the palace, trying to blend in with the crowd.

A short while later, they had finally got beyond the crowd and out of sight. Pearl led them over to the garden gate they had visited the previous day, whispering silently to Flutter. Flutter nodded and moved closer to the gate. She pulled out her now full bag of pixie dust and began to sprinkle it over the thick vines covering the gates.

Once again, the vines had turned into shades of beautiful, lush green. They unwrapped themselves from gates and slithered down to the ground like snakes. The gates opened, and Pearl, Lizzie and Diego stepped into the garden, the vines slipping back into place and the gates closing behind them.

Flutter and Diego slipped away as Lizzie, Pearl and Diego made their way through the gloomy garden. The plants were as dehydrated and lifeless as they were the day before, and the air was filled with the same sandy dust that covered the dry, dusty floor.

"I still don't get why these poor plants haven't been cared for. Why does Queen Sophie not like this beautiful place? Well, it used to be pretty anyway, as one of my books described it" Diego mentioned.

"Hmm… I never thought of that. Maybe this is linked to why she murdered her father. She surely must have loved him somehow" Lizzie agreed.

"Well, it could be. Good thinking! Ok, hurry up, we have to get in before lunch is over! C'mon!" Pearl ordered, rather hurriedly.

The three of them silently crept over to the door, ready to open it, only to discover that it was locked. "How are we supposed to get in now, the only proper secret entrance nearby is locked!"

“Why not check if there are any ways in through the air vents? Or why not look for windows? Maybe even a-”

“Rooftop! A hole in the wall! Anything!” Lizzie cut him off.

“Those are very foolish ideas! For now, until we come up with a plan or contact the other two, we’ll have to hide, because we could easily be spotted by a maid or a butler who could be simply looking out the window. Alright, let’s hide here. No one could see us out here from the windows”

The other two reluctantly agreed with Pearl and listened to her, for they knew she knew best. They hid in a playhouse which was part of the little playground in the garden. It was quite large, and so the three of them could easily fit inside. They sat down on the little chairs in the middle and began to discuss ideas of getting into the palace. Some were ridiculous, and others were far too obvious. They could just not find a proper way to enter the palace secretly!

A LITTLE HELP, PLEASE?

They furiously continued to squabble on and on about how they would get into the palace. No one seemed to have any sensible ideas, Pearl had argued earlier. They were arguing in quite a whisper, for they knew that they could easily be heard by a simple maid, or the Queen herself.

Thump. Thump. They were hearing loud footsteps coming from the garden door. From the small, tiny window they could see two little feet wearing black shoes, the coattail of a tuxedo, and a small white towel neatly folded at the creases. One of the butlers had come outside.

The three of them held their breaths and sat as still as statues. The butler came closer and closer until they heard a shrill voice yell "Antonio! That bush better be empty by the time the visitors leave! Her Majesty needs her evening berries. Without them, we're in big trouble! Now scram!"

What a coincidence! The strange butler was Antonio, whom they had met at the Queen's Dinner! They finally had a way in! Pearl nodded over to Lizzie, who was already getting ready to leave the playhouse, putting on hats, bracelets, and other accessories to disguise herself and make a dramatic appearance. Lizzie walked out of the playhouse and started, "Oh dear, my nephew is still missing, and I can't seem to find him anywhere. I'm pretty sure I saw him come out here!".

"Um... Madam, should I help you find your nephew? I know this garden inside out" Antonio politely asked, using his perfect butler etiquette as he approached the playhouse where three of them had hidden.

"Oh, that would be just wonderful of you! Show me everywhere he could be! Thank goodness you're here, butler"

Antonio walked with Lizzie around the garden, helping her look for her "Nephew". Lizzie led him as far away from the playground as possible, so Pearl and Diego had enough time to sneak in through the door. Lizzie, if possible, would follow in after she finished distracting Antonio in the garden.

Pearl and Diego waited for Lizzie to signal to them so that they knew they were safe to move. Lizzie turned around and signaled over to them that it was possible to enter. They crept up to the door, which had been left wide open by Antonio when he came out to pluck berries from a particular bush for Queen Sophie. Luckily, he didn't suspect a thing and went right along with Lizzie, who was still pretending to be upset by the fact that her nephew was missing, even though Antonio had been trying to console her the whole time.

"Oh, my poor darling, he must be suffering without me! Oh, why did he need to wander off without me, oh why!" Lizzie wailed.

"It's alright, Madam, we'll find your nephew in no time. He can't have gone too far from here, he'll have to be nearby" said Antonio, attempting to console Lizzie, who was still wailing about her "nephew", which seemed quite hard to do in the first place. Antonio continued to speak to a seemingly upset Lizzie, trying to calm her down and console her.

That gave Pearl and Diego the perfect opportunity to sneak in without being noticed. They got onto their tiptoes and silently crept in through the open door. The hallway was long and wide, and a scarlet carpet had been rolled out all along it. The walls had a warm glow from the beige color, making it feel nice and cozy.

"Now, if I remember, this is how pretty much all of the hallways here look, except for hallways with very important or secret rooms. Those hallways have blue carpets, grey walls, and they feel gloomy and spooky. We need to look for those hallways. Anyway, there aren't too many, so we should be able to find our target fast. Got it?" Pearl explained thoughtfully.

"I think so. But how do we get into one of these hallways in the first place? Like, won't there be any security measures? We could get caught, you know" Diego asked, unassured.

"Security measures? Pffft. Like the Queen has time to organize that. She never does that kinda stuff. Sophie is WAY too lazy to do that. No one can catch us, 'cos Sophie and most of the people here are near the convention, and so they can't hear or see us that easily. Ok, let's roll!"

The two of them followed their map down the hallways of the palace. Some were big and wide whilst others were small and narrow. Yet still, they all looked and felt the same, at least until they encountered their first importantly secret hallway.

The hallway was exactly the way Pearl had described it, except that it had one other thing. There was security. Pearl peeked over from behind the wall they were standing behind. Two guards were standing at each column at the beginning of the hallway. “Who's right now?” Diego asked Pearl, feeling quite satisfied with himself.

“Shh! Be quiet! We don't want those guards to hear us, right?” Pearl shushed him in a whisper.

“Alright, alright! Calm down, we can get past any obstacle, as we have done in the past. Now, what’s our plan?”

They whispered rapidly huddled together, but what they didn’t know was that the two guards were listening to them all this time. As Pearl peeked over to the guards, one of them was whispering silently into a Walkie-Talkie. She couldn’t exactly make out the words, but what she heard was something about a butler and a garden. She tried to put the pieces together, but it just didn’t make sense. Pearl had a strange feeling, and somehow sensed something familiar coming in sight.

Meanwhile, Flutter and Dwarfer were wandering around in the valley town, peeking in at shops and stands as they passed them. They even bought a few souvenirs from a couple of places, so they could keep some mementos from the mission. Dwarfer was eager to contact the other three on his Walkie-Talkie, but Flutter told him to be patient and wait until they were contacted by Pearl, Lizzie and Diego themselves.

"Oh, just let them get on with it, they'll probably just get caught if we disturb them with silly chatter!" Flutter argued.

Dwarfer put away his Walkie-Talkie with a heavy sigh. Walking around in the valley town wasn't as fun without all of his friends, let alone not even being allowed to chat with them. He and Flutter walked on through the beautiful, narrow streets. There wasn't much to enjoy anyway, so why not just take a beautiful stroll to pass the time, thought Dwarfer.

Meanwhile, Lizzie and Antonio had almost reached one end of the garden. Lizzie had managed to distract him pretending to be upset about her missing "nephew" for the fifteen-minute-long walk and as she approached a side of the fence, she decided that she was going to tell Antonio about the real reason she had approached him. Antonio had proven himself trustworthy in all the favors he had already done for the team. It was the right decision to make.

"Antonio, can I tell you something?" Lizzie politely asked, revealing herself from underneath her hat.

"HOLD ON! You're that Miss Shelley from Rodney's!" Antonio exclaimed.

"Yes, that's me. I'll tell you everything, but you have to promise me that you won't tell a single soul. You've got to promise me"

"Well, if you're going to explain about all this, then you'd better get on with it. I won't be telling anyone anyway"

"Alright. So, first things first, my name is Lizzie Thomas, not Miss Shelley. I'm here on a mission, and don't worry, I'll get to that bit in a second" Lizzie began.

"You'd better!"

"Of course, I will! I always keep to my promises!" .

Lizzie told him all about how she got here, when she met Pearl and the others, about the Just Soc, Damien, and the inn, their mission idea and pretty much everything else. Antonio was astonished. He almost couldn't believe it.

"So, all of this happened in such a short amount of time? That is extraordinary! Your ideas are certainly amazing! I have one question. Do you happen to be related to Elizabeth the brave, one of Fantasia's most valued Heroes?" Antonio asked, plenty of excitement bubbling inside him.

"Thank you for all the compliments. And yes, I do happen to be related to Elizabeth Thomas. She is my Gran. I also obviously know that she is one of Fantasia's most important heroes" Lizzie replied politely.

"No wonder you are of such excellence, Madam! Your Grandmother has been such a great influence on your great ideas" Antonio squeaked.

"You don't need to do all the fancy butler stuff. Now what I need is your help. If you could do me a favor and help us to get to the computer room, that would be great!" Lizzie told him.

"O...o...of c...c...course! I am honored to help you in any way you can with your magnificent plan. It is certainly time to stop the Queen from her evil activities and most possibly end her regime! Now that would be splendid for us servants and workers, for she treats us like old little rags. There are a few particular servants she likes, her favorites, and she always lets them off and gives someone else the blame and punishment for what they did. That annoys those of us who always end up doing the dirty work. Anyway, let's get back to your favor. I have just the plan!"

Lizzie listened carefully as Antonio described his masterful plan to get to the computers. Antonio would sneak Lizzie into the staff room and convince his boss to let them guard one of the very important forbidden hallways. Since the computers lay amongst one of those hallways, it would be much easier to find Pearl and Diego, because they'd be looking for the computers in that area. The rest of the plan was the same as Lizzie and the team had already discussed.

"Finally, someone truthful who is willing to help us. We needed a little bit of help" Lizzie sighed happily.

HALLWAY MAZE

Before they executed their plan, Antonio quickly plucked off some berries for the Queen. He then walked over to the door silently, motioning for Lizzie to follow him. They crept through the silent hallways, occasionally hiding behind pillars or curtains when a servant or maid was approaching. At last, after a lot of creeping around and hiding, they finally reached the door marked “Staffroom”. Antonio slowly pushed open the door to check if anyone was there, and to their luck, no one was there.

The staff room was filled with trays and bins full of supplies, uniforms, and whatnot. They were going to put on the security uniforms, then wait until Antonio’s boss arrived so they could get assigned to patrol the forbidden hallways. From then on, everything would be much easier.

Lizzie and Antonio found plenty of uniforms in the bins. Lizzie picked up two blue jumpsuits with the words “Royal security” and the Royal Crest embroidered on either side. “These must be the Security uniforms we’ve been looking for!” Lizzie triumphantly exclaimed.

"I assume so. I advise that we hurry up and put these on before my boss gets here and recognizes the fact that you aren't one of our staff members. It wouldn't be nice for either of us if we got caught." said Antonio.

The two of them slipped into the jumpsuits, took off their accessories, and hid them away. Lizzie found two "Royal Security" hats, and so in place of their normal accessories, they wore the blue hats, which had the same embroideries as the jumpsuit on it.

"These must be part of our Security Guard uniforms!" Lizzie had pointed out when she found them.

"Hurry up, we've got to put them on because if we don't, someone might find out that we aren't here to do work. And as I said, we can't get caught" Antonio reminded her.

They both put the hats on. Lizzie thought that the uniform was quite comfy. On the contrary, Antonio hated it. He bounced around the room, itching like crazy. Lizzie just laughed and commented. "You look like someone who doesn't belong here. Ooh, I know! You look like a monkey! Here little monkey, here's a banana! It's all yours!" she teased.

“Not funny! Not funny at ALL!” Antonio scowled, annoyed by Lizzie’s teasing. Lizzie just laughed. All of a sudden, the door slammed open, and a big, athletic man appeared through the doorway. He wasn’t just big. He was humongous.

“What’re ‘you lazy lot doin’ in here, eh? Security aren’t yeh?” he barked.

“Y…y…yes boss, we are security. We just c…c…came in to get ready for our shift” Antonio stammered, pretending to be scared.

“Well, wherever you’re supposed to be patrolling can wait. The Queen raised an urgent security post, and you’ll be patrolling there”

“M…m…may we ask w…w…where we need to patrol?” Lizzie and Antonio stammered and stumbled one after the other convincingly.

“All I know is that you’re supposed to be patrolling the forbidden hallways. Hurry up and get over there. And stay there for the next two hours. Got it?”

“O…o…ok boss. We will finish the assigned t…t…task on t…t…time for you. Y…y…you can count on us”

“Now get out! I don’t want to see you here for the next two hours! Scram!” shouted Antonio’s very impatient and rude boss.

The two of them then pretended to be scared and ran out of the door as fast as they could. Antonio dragged Lizzie away from the staff rooms so that they could have a quick conversation.

"Just so you know, the stammering was just for dramatic effect. That makes it much more believable for a boss like mine" Antonio mentioned.

"Oh, I know! Some things are obvious in life, you should know!" Lizzie snapped angrily.

"And all of a sudden you're starting to snap at me. Why is that so? Did I say anything bad? You can tell me, you know!"

Lizzie heaved a sigh. "Oh, it's just, you know, there's something nagging at me and I just can't seem to figure it out. It kind of got me frustrated, and now I'm just feeling annoyed. Have you ever felt like that?"

Antonio didn't know what to say. "Hmm... Hang on. Tell me, what's been nagging at you. Maybe I can help? Then it'll hopefully become less frustrating for you" Antonio said, in an attempt to help Lizzie.

"Never mind, time isn't on our side now, and we've got to get going, since we don't have a map of the palace, and you don't know where the forbidden hallways are anyway. We'll talk about it later" Lizzie said, pushing him away.

"Ok, so which way should we go? Straight, Back, Right, or Left?"

"How should I know? You're the one who knows this place the best out of the two of us" Lizzie reminded him sternly.

"Ok, ok. I say we go... Left! It's because one of the hallways on this side has a room which I think could be useful for us to get to the forbidden hallways. Come on!"

The two of them walked through the long hallway, all the way until the end. "I believe this is the right one. Follow me, Lizzie!"

"Ooookay, if you say so. I'm trusting you to lead us the right way, so this better not be wrong"

Antonio gulped. What would happen if he got it wrong? He led Lizzie through another long hallway, anxiously looking at every door and reading its label. "Oh yes! Um, we don't need to go to the room I was looking for, because I remember learning the way to the forbidden hallways!" Antonio explained to Lizzie about his excuse, which seemed quite believable to Lizzie anyhow because he wasn't able to find the room that he was looking for anywhere in the long hallway they had just walked through.

"That's better! Now we'll have more time to get there! Good job for remembering, Antonio, I'm impressed!"

"Uh...thanks, I guess? Anyways, let's get going, uh...before we lose our uh...extra time!"

"Alright, lead the way, Antonio! It's time to pick up the pace!" Lizzie agreed, nodding approvingly.

Antonio led Lizzie along a few more hallways, pretending that he was quite confident about the way they were heading. However, in reality, Antonio had no idea where he was leading the both of them, so he just hoped that it would bring them somehow to the forbidden hallways.

"So, exactly how far are we from our destination again?" asked Lizzie curiously.

"We um... are not too far, I assume. The forbidden hallways are probably somewhere close by, I uh... assure you" Antonio hurriedly replied.

"Well, that's good! Keep me updated, I'll be looking out for anyone who could be watching or listening to us, okay?"

They continued to walk along, following Antonio's lead. The farther they went, the more guilty Antonio felt. He didn't want to leave Lizzie there alone, but he also didn't want to mislead her by doing the wrong thing. I'm going to come clean, thought Antonio.

After a few minutes of hard thinking, Antonio took a deep breath and asked Lizzie awkwardly "Hey, can I um... uh... tell you um... something?".

"Sure! Go ah...".

"I don't know where we're going because I couldn't find the room we were looking for and so I didn't want you to get super-duper mad at me and… lock me up in the dungeons!" Antonio blurted, interrupting Lizzie.

"You thought I would, like, imprison you in the dungeons? No way! You're a trustworthy person, and that's why I told you this. No one is expecting you to be perfect, you know! It's ok, we'll figure it out somehow"

"Th…th…thanks"

"You can always rely on me for help," Lizzie told Antonio cheerily. He nodded. Lizzie grabbed Antonio's hand and started to run. She dragged him speedily through the hallways, causing him to bump upon the ground violently. "This… is… PAINFUL!" Antonio shrieked in pain, hoping that Lizzie would slow down a little.

Lizzie just continued speeding through the hallways. It was as if the two of them were just large gusts of wind passing by. "Awesome, right?" Lizzie asked. Antonio nodded in pain, attempting to smile.

They sped through many hallways, looking out for anything of blue color. Lizzie suddenly came to a halt. "Phew! That's over"

"Well, that's a complicated hallway maze," Antonio said with a laugh.

GUARDS IN DISGUISE

Now that they had reached their destination, Lizzie and Antonio were not so sure about what they were supposed to do. Antonio had suggested guarding the hallways like they were supposed to do, but Lizzie said that the real reason they were here was to find the computer room and turned his idea down.

"Then what on earth are you planning to do? Do you have any idea, huh?" Antonio asked impatiently.

"Well, I think I might have one, but I don't know if it's a good idea"

"Every idea is worth a try. Go on, tell me about this idea..."

Lizzie shrugged. "Okay, but don't tell me that I didn't warn you if anything goes wrong," she said, agreeing.

The two of them got into position in the large, roomy hallway, and waited for the right time to get into action. Lizzie and Antonio chatted casually, making them sound like actual palace guards. They were walking back and forth, to make sure that they were keeping track of every single thing around them.

"They should be here at some point, they can't take forever to get here!" Lizzie whined impatiently, annoyed that nothing was happening.

"Shh, calm down, they're bound to get here soon, you know?"

"Well, they even have a map, and yet they're taking so long! That's just really getting on my nerves today!"

"So, what, uh..., well, you do have a point there, I should say" Antonio agreed hesitantly.

"See what I mean!" Lizzie shouted at him annoyedly.

"Ooookay, no need to get so mad about it, Lizzie. Just calm down, as I told you earlier"

"Fine, but they better get here soon, or else I won't hold it anymore"

Lizzie and Antonio had been waiting for what seemed like a decade. They were about to give up and leave, just as a strange buzzing noise came from nowhere. "What an awful noise!" Antonio complained.

Lizzie pulled out her Walkie-Talkie from her pocket. "You mean this? Oh, it just means someone is trying to contact me" Lizzie whispered, pointing at the small device she held.

Lizzie pressed the connection button on her Walkie-Talkie and whispered "Hello? Anyone there?".

"Um, hey Lizzie, Branch speaking. Any updates on the mission yet?"

"Let me see, hmm... we've found Flutter, we reached the palace, and now we're looking for the computer room. I think that's pretty much it, I'm guessing"

"Ok, just connect when you're ready. I have one question though. Why are you whispering?"

"Maybe because we probably can't let anyone hear us?" Lizzie snapped.

"Shhh, we have to be quiet, Lizzie!"

"W...w...who is that? D...d...do we know them? O...o...over" Branch stammered, frightened, and shocked by the new voice.

"Hold on, I'll explain all of that later"

"Okay," said Branch. Lizzie told her about Rodneys, the gala dinner, Bethilda, The Ranch, and more. Antonio was patiently looking out for anything unusual, whilst Lizzie explained everything to Branch.

Just as Lizzie was getting to the part where they found Antonio on his butler duty in the castle garden, Antonio noticed two figures peeking over from behind the wall upfront. He immediately recognized them as Diego and Pearl, remembering their appearances from the times he had met them. He walked over to Lizzie, who was still not finished with her epic storytelling and nudged her gently.

"What now? What is so ridiculously important that you need to disturb me? Can't you see that I'm busy explaining everything to Branch here, who is patiently listening to me, even if she needs to get back to work!" Lizzie snapped at him angrily.

"Woah, calm down. We can move forward and head to the computer room if you listen to me. It's them, they're here. Look, there they are, behind that wall in front of us. We should make sure that they don't pass us, or this plan will be a total failure!" Antonio whisper-shouted, obviously annoyed that Lizzie was snapping at him unnecessarily.

"I see. You keep an eye on them for now, I'll just finish my little story here and I'll be right with you. Is that alright?" Lizzie requested, turning away from the Walkie-Talkie to pay attention to what Antonio had said. Antonio nodded agreeingly. Lizzie then continued to recite all the information they had gained throughout the journey to Branch, who was listening patiently on the other end, whilst Antonio kept looking out for Pearl and Diego.

Pearl and Diego were wondering how to get past those guards in their way, little did they know that these guards were just Lizzie and Antonio in disguise, so that they could go back to work and complete their mission together.

“I still don’t have any idea of how we’ll get past those guards without them noticing us. Have you got any ideas in mind? We could really use them right now” Diego asked.

“No, I don’t have any ideas either. Unless you want to come clean to the guards, I don’t see how we’ll be able to get past them without getting noticed” Pearl responded.

“Hmm...In that case, I suggest that we pretend that we are two staff members coming to get something for the Queen. It’s the only idea I could think of now”

“I suppose it’s worth a try since none of us have any other sensible or possible ideas in place. Now, we should probably come up with a dialogue that seems convincing enough to the guards, otherwise, we could be easily caught by them”

“That’s fair enough. Of course, we always need to make sure that we are very careful about the tracks we leave behind. I already have a very convincing dialogue, and I am pretty sure that will work out well. Let’s start!” Diego chattered, bursting with plenty of new ideas as he usually did.

The both of them practiced their convincing dialogues when they went past the guards in a soft, quiet whisper. Antonio listened in to their little conversation and practices, waiting for them to come out of hiding and begin their dialogue show. He peeked over at Diego from the corner of his eye, for the first time noticing how smart his idea was.

"Maybe this boy is much more intelligent, clever and useful than I thought he was in the first place. You can never be too knowledgeable in terms of great ideas and valuable information!" Antonio admitted truthfully to Lizzie, truly amazed by young Diego's wide variety of information he knew about.

"You never believed me until now? Hmph! That is unbelievable! Oh fine, it is believable because not a single person yet has believed me when I told them about Diego and his amazing intelligence until they meet him and get to know him! So don't think that I'm mad at you, ok?" Lizzie fired at him, fuming with rage and immediately cooling down, recalling past incidents with the same problem each time.

"So, what now! I told you, now I believe you completely and I know that Diego is quite Smart for an 8-year-old boy!" Antonio argued, losing his cool because he was fed up with all the arguments Lizzie kept starting, each time just because there was a little, unimportant matter.

"Whatever, just forget about it. Besides, we don't have time to waste on silly arguments anyhow, right?" Antonio calmed himself down and ended the argument from his side. Lizzie nodded, which meant that their little squabble was over.

The two of them watched as Pearl and Diego continuously practiced in a silent whisper, trying to be as convincing as possible. After what seemed like an eternity, Pearl and Diego were finally done practicing to be as convincing as possible for the guards. Pearl nodded over to Diego. They then strode over, attempting to appear as posh and responsible as possible to the guards.

"What do you think you're doing here, you two?" Antonio questioned, in an attempt to make himself appear as Guard-like as much as he could.

"Oh, it's me, Princess Pearl, and this is the nephew of my assistant, Miss Shelley. She told me that we would meet in the lunchroom later, but I couldn't find her, and instead, I found-" Pearl started her dialogue.

"Just kidding! Pearl, it's me, Lizzie, and the other Guard is Antonio! Now come on, we haven't got any time to lose"

"Wow! How did you even get such awesome costumes? How did you even get here? I've got so much to ask!"

"As I said Diego, we've got no time to lose, just wait! I'll explain everything later when we have time!" Lizzie reminded him. The others nodded in agreement, they would listen to the whole story of their mission after all stages of their masterful plan to defeat Queen Sophie and end her reign until order was restored in the kingdom of Fantasia once again.

The group of four was about to start sprinting through the hallways, but just about then, Lizzie realized that sprinting wasn't probably the best idea. "Wait, guys! Sprinting is probably not the best idea, because Antonio and I could easily get caught, guards aren't supposed to be running on their shifts at all! Let's try walking quietly at a normal pace. Maybe that would be less obvious?" She mentioned.

"You have learned how to be proper guards in disguise!" laughed Pearl.

THE SECRET COMPUTER ROOM

The group walked down hallways, reading each door label to make sure they hadn't missed anything useful for their mission. Occasionally they saw a servant or two, but they managed to jump behind a plant or hide behind one of the blue curtains just in time. Luckily, so far, none of them had been seen, as far as they knew and had observed.

At one point, a maid unexpectedly walked into the hallway the group was in. Pearl was able to jump behind a tall plant, Diego skittered behind one of the curtains and Lizzie squeezed herself into a small gap between a few barrels. However, Antonio couldn't find a single place to hide, and before he knew it, the maid had walked into the hallway he was standing in.

Luckily, Antonio was wearing the guard's uniform and so he was able to pretend that he had been assigned to a guard's post in the hallway he was standing in. The maid passed by him, staring at him in an unsure manner. She took her time to roll the cart along the hallway, still staring at Antonio at his guard's post even as she walked away to the next hallway. After what seemed like the longest wait ever, the maid and her cart were finally out of sight and a safe distance away from them.

"Phew! That was close! I almost thought I wouldn't make it without getting caught!" Antonio whispered in relief.

"You are most certainly right! I was so terrified that we were going to get caught! However luckily you managed to pull it off, so congratulations, Agent Antonio!" Pearl beamed at him with pride and delight.

"Well, uh…um thank you, I suppose?"

"There is no need to be standing around here now, you two. Hop along! We must hurry, before anything changes!" Lizzie interrupted, annoyed that they were simply just slowing all of them down on the mission they were working to accomplish, and with that, she went back to reading the label on one of the many doors in the Queen's palace. Pearl and Antonio stayed put and continued chatting there, whilst Diego kept on telling them to come with him to help Lizzie.

"Oh, come on! We really do have to go now, so stop standing around!" said Diego in agreement with Lizzie's argument.

Pearl and Antonio pretended to not have heard him and continued to chatter on about some of the topics they both knew a lot about, surprisingly they had many shared interests. Lizzie kept giving them looks as they searched along the hallways that said, stop-now-or-else, but that didn't change their minds at all.

Diego tried to interrupt them by making awkward noises in between their sentences, but that only made them get more engaged in their conversation. A few minutes later, Lizzie got so mad about Pearl and Antonio neglecting what she and Diego were trying to tell them, she began to glare at them with so much fury that Pearl noticed almost immediately and nudged Diego gently with her elbow.

"Finally! You are noticing that we are still here waiting for you to help us! Now, I am sure that we will probably find the secret computer room in one of the next few hallways. So, let's hurry and get this over with" Diego told Pearl in response to her nudge.

"That wasn't the reason I called for your attention. I was wondering why Lizzie is just glaring at us, well, me and Antonio so furiously, and I thought that you would probably have the answer to my question" Pearl explained.

"Easy. She is doing that because she is quite mad at you both for wasting precious mission time talking about something utterly irrelevant. That's a pretty simple reason if you ask me. It is quite normal and reasonable that Lizzie is mad at you both, and I suggest that we'd better go and help her"

"Fine, if you insist. We'll come with you and help you with finding the right door, even if you probably could easily find it without us"

"I don't think that will be necessary at all. Come and look!" Lizzie said.

Pearl gasped. "No way, you found it! Great Job Lizzie!" she exclaimed.

Antonio decided to stand guard in the hallway just in case anyone approached them. Diego attempted to open the door, only to realize that the Queen wouldn't keep the door to the computer room unlocked. He then pulled out a hairpin from his pocket, bent it around a little, and then stuck it in the keyhole to unlock the door. Unsurprisingly, it worked, and they could now enter the computer room.

The room that Pearl, Lizzie, and Diego stepped into was dimly lit, and for the three of them, it seemed quite cramped. Diego pulled out a flashlight from his pocket and turned the little black switch on. Suddenly, the room was filled with bright light, just enough so that they could properly see the items stored in the computer room.

Lizzie noticed many large monitors and keyboards set up inside. There were also a few odd-looking bits of machinery that none of them could recognize clearly at first sight. Apart from that, there were only a few other things in the room such as piles of books, papers, a few tables, and chairs.

"I don't see how you three are going to do anything with this stuff. I don't know what is in this room" Antonio complained confusedly.

"Antonio! I already told you, in the computer room, the Queen has stored all of her past and future plans. With this information, we can easily always be ahead of her and beat her at her own game, although anyway, we still need to figure out what that is" Lizzie explained to him once more shortly.

"Oh! Now I get it! That does make sense, but I still don't know how you are going to do it anyhow"

"Well, we don't have any time to explain right now, so you might as well hop along and pretend that you are guarding the hallways. I'll explain to you what we did later" Lizzie told him. Antonio nodded and began pacing up and down the long hallway.

"Now you do look like a guard who is doing his work!" Pearl commented, giggling quietly.

By then, Diego had reached the monitors and began to turn them on. He drummed his fingers on the table as he waited for the machine to finish booting up. Once they were all on, he realized something. He typed something on the keyboard, only to see that it wasn't of any use.

Diego called over Pearl and Lizzie. He told them sternly "I don't know how, but we forgot about one of the most challenging obstacles in this room. The password".

PASSWORD

Lizzie recalled, “We never even talked about any kind of password in the computer room”.

“Well, you are right, but I do remember Queen Sophie telling us on the tour of her palace that there are passwords on devices in the computer room. Unfortunately, she didn’t say anything else, so I can’t help you too much” Pearl added, pointing out the fact that neither she had any idea about the password.

“Okay, we are nowhere near finding out how to unlock these monitors. For once, I don’t want it to be me who has to come up with the perfect solution like every other time. You guys have great ideas too!” Diego stated.

The three of them stood a while thinking. They searched their minds for a reasonable idea, but at first, they could only come up with some part of an idea instead of an idea as a whole.

“I have an idea, but before we can implement it, we need to figure out how we are going to make it part of a bigger solution” Pearl described her idea thoughtfully, unsure about how it could be helpful at all.

"Same here. I just can't see how these little parts can make a perfect solution in the first place" Lizzie complained about the situation.

"Wait! What if we put all our ideas together to make the perfect solution to our situation? Wouldn't that just be great!" Diego suggested.

The group thought about it together. "True, Diego. It could work if we did it as a team" Lizzie agreed.

"Hmm... I suppose so, but if it doesn't work, there is nothing we can do, and you shouldn't blame anyone for that" Pearl commented hesitantly.

"So, we all agree. We'll put our ideas together and then figure out how we are going to crack the code. Let's give it a go!" Diego cheerily told them.

They shared their ideas and almost immediately got to work on the monitors, starting with the one closest to the door. Since there were three monitors, they would have to work on one at a time.

Their overall idea was to try out combinations of regular things in the palace or part of Queen Sophie's life. One of them would search around the room for clues to the password if they were hidden in anyplace. The others would try different combinations on the monitor until a clue was found. Lastly, they would use the clue to discover the password, and then they would return to their established plan.

"It's quite a simple plan, I must say" Lizzie pointed out.

"Easier said than done" Pearl and Diego both replied in chorus.

Lizzie went to look for any clues that were hidden around the room. Pearl and Diego turned to one of the monitors and began typing in random password combinations. Pearl instructed Diego to type the combinations since he was quite experienced with technology and could type fast. They tried out combinations of words such as "Sophie Queen" or "White Queen". However, those combinations were nowhere near the correct one.

They even tried random numerical combinations, "24.07" or "365.12". Diego quickly tapped the number keys for each combination and then waited for the monitor to finish loading the result onto the screen. However, that didn't help them find the right password either.

"Have you guys worked out the correct password yet? I am getting bored looking for clues because there is nothing in this room that will help us to find the password, and there is nothing to search in the first place" Lizzie whined.

Diego looked up to Pearl. Pearl sighed and answered her "No, not really. You see, in royal palaces, people don't keep things simple. It's all very complicated. That's why we can't find the password so easily in the first place! So, my answer is no, we are nowhere near it".

"Now, that seems so great, so great that I give up on looking for any clues! I will do anything but that"

"You don't need to get so hyped up about that. Things aren't as easy as you think in Fantasia, and it's time that you knew that properly. There could be clues hidden in the least obvious places, who knows?"

"Hmph! Fine, if you say so. Anyway, why would they even hide clues in the palace? Is it like they want people to find out their secrets?"

"I don't know, there isn't a specific reason for why they do that here. It's just like that, they just do things that way" Pearl shrugged and answered.

“Whatever. There is a reason for everything, so there must be a reason why Queen Sophie hid clues in the computer room to find the password and I declare that we go and find out why she did that” Lizzie ordered.

“No, we have to figure out the password to these monitors, otherwise we are going to be delayed in our mission! We can’t just let everyone down now” Diego reminded her.

“You know what? You are right. I’ll go back to searching for clues and you guys do whatever you were doing. I am sure we will find a solution to all this in the end”

“Fine by me. Diego, try the combinations that I am going to tell you” Pearl instructed.

So, the three of them went back to work, trying endlessly to find out the password. That went on for quite a long time, none of them coming up with any possible solutions. By the time an hour had passed, they were all tired of attempting for so long to find the password. Diego almost fell asleep whilst typing up the combinations, Pearl almost lost her voice by telling Diego what to type and Lizzie was about to faint because she had searched every nook and cranny of the room multiple times, but only ended up with nothing.

Suddenly, Lizzie's mood lightened up. She had just thought of something that could possibly lead them to the correct password. Pearl and Diego sat at the monitors, watching Lizzie as she paced back and forth around the room. She was in a state of deep thought, coming up with an idea that would most probably be one of the best she ever had.

"Pearl, what is Queen Sophie like? What kind of personality does she have?" Lizzie questioned.

"Honestly, she is a bit selfish and very rude. Sophie also is quite forgetful, she just sometimes can't remember things. She keeps lots of hidden reminders... ohhh! I see what you're getting at!" Pearl answered, understanding what Lizzie had in mind. Diego too had understood Lizzie's point, using his intelligence to figure it out.

"So, are any of you going to help me pick the lock on the closet door? Come on, hurry up! Remember, we don't have much time!"

Pearl pulled out her hairpin and handed it over to Diego, who was already getting ready to pull out another trick from up his sleeve to open up the closet door. Diego stepped over to the lock, and with a simple turn in it, the lock and the closet were both open. Lizzie and Pearl just stood there staring at the open closet.

"What are we waiting for! Let's look for this password reminder!" Diego exclaimed excitedly, making sure that Lizzie and Pearl were paying attention to him even if they were still staring at the open closet.

Diego began searching the closet for Queen Sophie's password reminder. Eventually, after a few minutes, Pearl and Lizzie joined him and looked in the other corners of the closet. At first, they looked in the most obvious places, realizing that Queen Sophie probably wouldn't hide her reminders in places where people could easily get hold of them and spoil her plans.

The three of them looked carefully in every nook and cranny of the closet. The closet was quite large, and it had a lot of space for storage. As they searched, they came across documents such as yearly tax bills or newspaper articles. These documents were probably connected to the information that they would find in the computer room, Lizzie thought.

As Diego was looking at the far-right end of the closet, he came across a drawer. He pulled it open and checked if there was a false bottom. There was indeed! He pulled it out, revealing a small piece of paper that had been folded multiple times. Diego picked it up and announced triumphantly "I found it first! It was in a drawer with the false bottom, how easy to find!".

"Easy for you, not so much for us, you should know" Lizzie scoffed annoyedly, but with the hint of relief that they had found the password at last.

Diego ignored her and unfolded the little piece of paper completely. He read the words "ARCHIVE MONITOR PASSWORD: **password**" out loud.

"Seriously, she kept the password that simple!?! We couldn't even figure that out!" Lizzie complained.

"That was pretty clever of her. But anyway, for someone that forgetful, that password would have to be simple so that one could remember" Pearl mentioned.

"Hmm...True, you do have a point, and that does make sense, because the way you described her, Queen Sophie seems like quite a careless person to me"

Diego exclaimed, "What are we standing around for in the first place! Let's go type in the password!".

VALUABLE INFORMATION

They all rushed to the monitors and waited for Diego to type in the code on all three keyboards. He pressed ENTER crossing his fingers as he did so. After two or three minutes of waiting, the words "Welcome Sophie" were displayed on the screen, with a series of files on the main desktop to accompany it.

"Are you both thinking what I am thinking?" Lizzie squealed once she saw the desktop screen.

"File search! Let's dig through and find what we need!" Diego and Pearl both replied with plenty of enthusiasm and excitement.

The three of them madly rushed through the files on each of the monitors in front of them. Most of them were empty and useless, and as minutes passed by, Pearl, Diego, and Lizzie were getting tired of searching through many empty folders and files.

"I feel like the computer room is just a trick, and Queen Sophie will trap us" Lizzie complained, slowly losing faith in their plan.

"Trust me, my calculations of this plan are 101% sure and it isn't a trick. My instincts are telling me that these multiple empty folders and files are just to make the real archive more hidden and protected. Let's search for other applications on the monitor" Diego informed her reassuringly.

"Diego is right. Sophie wouldn't keep anything in her palace that was easy to find. If it was, she would change it and make it more hidden and harder to discover" Pearl briefly explained, agreeing with Diego.

They began to check the other applications that were installed on the monitors. Lizzie scrolled up and down with the mouse, Diego typed with a click-clack on the keyboard and Pearl kept on clicking everything in her sight. However, the little group of three were yet to find exactly what they were looking for.

Pearl and Diego had just finished searching thoroughly through each application installed on the computer they were able to find. Lizzie was just finishing off the search in the last application, as she came across a little icon popping around her screen. The icon was about the size of an eraser, and it was designed to look like a locked metal safe. She tried to drag it away from the screen, but the little icon kept on reappearing, frustrating Lizzie more and more each time she tried.

Lizzie became bored of trying to get rid of the icon, so she clicked on it, hoping that it would disappear. Instead, she was led to a completely different page. The page showed a loading sign, which was already halfway done. Lizzie was confused. She tried to click around the screen, but nothing happened. The screen was stuck on the mysterious page.

"Diego, Pearl, you've got to see this. I clicked on this weird icon that kept on popping up, and now it led me to this page. I don't know what it is, and I think I might need both of you to help me figure it out" Lizzie explained, very panicked because of the mysterious and unknown icon she had clicked on.

"Oh, don't worry, it can't be that bad, for sure? If it really is terrible then we'll surely find a way to fix it, whatever it is" Diego reassured.

Lizzie tried to smile, but the worried expression she was wearing hadn't changed a bit.

"But anyway, let me take a look and see if I can help. You can never be sure about anything!" Diego added, making sure that the worried expression on Lizzie's face had disappeared.

Diego pushed his chair over to Lizzie's Monitor and sat down. He took a closer look at the page that was loading up in front of him on the screen. By then, the page showed 75% loaded. Strangely, Diego somehow was not able to recognize nor identify the type of page that the screen was currently displaying.

"Huh. This is strange software, and I have no clue about it. No wonder you looked so panicky!" Diego wondered loudly.

"So, since Diego has no clue about what we're dealing with, I think that we should probably wait and see what this little icon is," Pearl suggested.

By the time Pearl had finished with her suggestion, the loading bar had gone up to 99%. The three of them anxiously watched the almost blank screen, waiting rather impatiently for it to show 100% on the loading bar. After a few long minutes, the page displayed the words "100% Complete

All of a sudden, the screen went completely white. Lizzie, Diego, and Pearl had no clue about what they were going to do with the blank, useless screen they saw in front of them. "Well, I guess we've failed at finding the computer room. We might as well give up and go" Pearl said.

“Come on, Pearl, we’ve come this far, and we can’t give up at this point anymore. Let’s just wait and see what happens, just as you suggested” Lizzie said, trying to bring some positive vibes to the room, although even she felt quite deflated.

Pearl, Lizzie, and Diego continued to stare at the monitor, almost as still and quiet as statues. They were all concentrated on the blank screen, waiting for something to happen. After a while of doing so, the screen suddenly flashed multiple times and on the last flash, the monitor displayed a short title, which strangely enough, was the color of the red Ruby on Lizzie’s amulet.

“Woah! What on earth was that? Look, there is something new written on the screen! Let’s check it out and see what it says!” Lizzie noticed.

Diego bent over closer to the monitor and read “Welcome to your secret files, please click on a folder to continue”.

“Believe it or not guys, we just found the secret files! We are almost done with our mission! Way to go!” Diego cheered. The three of them high-fived and hugged each other for their great teamwork.

"Okay, okay, calm down guys. We may have found the secret files, but time to get to actual work. Whoever has the Walkie-Talkie and the special device attachment that we were given by the team who created it, get it out and give it to me, since I am going to contact them and get the data transfer process to start. Meanwhile, each one of you should probably login to the file area on the other and begin reading the files that are there. Maybe that way we will have more useful information against the Queen. By gaining more knowledge against Sophie, we will be able to turn everyone against her and stop her from ruining Fantasia. That's why I need you to work on that while I transfer the data to HQ. Understood?" Pearl instructed, making sure they were back on track to finish their mission successfully.

Diego and Lizzie nodded and pulled out the Walkie-Talkie and the special device Pearl had asked for. Then the both of them got work on digging up more information.

Pearl clicked her way to the correct channel on her Walkie-Talkie. Once she found the HQ's channel, she quickly dialed in to contact those at HQ. "Hello, HQ? We are ready to begin. Give me instructions on what to do so that the process can be started." Pearl informed, trying to get the attention of those at HQ.

The first one to hear Pearl's voice coming from the Walkie-Talkie was Lora, the leader of the tech team. She almost immediately jumped out of her seat and went to answer Pearl.

"Hi, Tech Lead speaking. Yes, we are all prepared to start the process. I need you to turn on the device provided and connect to the Database. This can be done through the Settings application." Lora replied to Pearl's announcement.

"Ok, working on it. Finished. Next step please!" Pearl said, doing exactly what Lora had instructed her to do as she talked. This went on for a while, Lora telling Pearl what to do so they could begin the data transfer. In the middle, Cooper joined them and helped Lora and Pearl with the technical parts of the transfer.

Whilst that was going on, Lizzie and Diego had opened the file area on the other monitors and had begun to read the files that had been stored on the file area. They were searching for any seemingly useful information, but they weren't able to find much.

"This is getting boring. I mean, who wants to read about how Queen Sophie has so many features making her look like a replica of Snow White? I feel like there is nothing important in her anymore. It's useless to continue searching if we won't find anything that will help us. Nothing is in my favor today. Nothing! That just irritates me so much!" Lizzie argued, annoyed that nothing had been going her way that day.

"Just search in another file. You'll surely find something or another if you look everywhere. And no, not everything isn't in your favor today! Look, we found the secret files and we were able to open them, thanks to you and we weren't caught at all" Diego told her, already knowing how to react to Lizzie's negative mood.

"Well, I suppose you do have a point, so I will give it a go, just so that we can get this over with. Alright, are you satisfied now?" Lizzie hesitantly replied to what Diego had told her. So, they continued reading different files, in search of important information.

Lizzie was skimming through the information in a file labeled "PLAN" as she came across something interesting. She couldn't believe what she had just read. "Bingo! Now, this is some valuable information against Queen Sophie" Lizzie triumphantly announced.

POWER TO CONQUER

Diego got up from his seat to go and see what Lizzie was talking about. When he read the information he saw on the screen, he gasped with excitement. "Woah, that is dangerous! Good thing we found out about this cruel act! That is great to know because now we can stop Sophie's evil plans and save Fantasia!" Diego cheered, happy to know what they were up against so that they could prepare themselves.

Pearl was confused by what Diego and Lizzie said. "Hold on, I need to clarify something with the team along with my, be right back. Over" Pearl said through the Walkie-Talkie to those at back HQ. Lora replied, saying that she would be waiting for her to finish on the line.

"What on Earth is all this fuss about! I would like to know, so is anyone going to explain this to me now?" Pearl asked confusedly, not sure what anyone meant by all the voices she had heard.

"Come and see for yourself! Not everything can be explained! All I can tell you is that we found some useful information from the secret files over here!" Diego told her, pretty sure that it would be better for Pearl to digest the information herself.

"Okay, I'll come to check it out, but this better not be a false alarm, or I'm going to get really mad" Pearl agreed warningly, already assuming that she would probably find nothing useful in the information found by Lizzie and Diego, and she was just wasting her time by going to check it out. However, once she had finished reading the little groups of text on the bright display, Pearl was astonished. This information was the answer to many of her questions about Queen Sophie's strangest orders and ideas.

"Wow! That is super dangerous! We can't let Sophie do this to Fantasia! I however do have some important points to consider, which I have used the information we just found to confirm. Let me just finish my conversation with HQ and then I will explain to both of you what I mean. You can come along with me and talk with those at HQ for a bit since you probably checked all other files, I assume. Alright, understood?" Pearl chattered excitedly, her mood had changed since she read the archive file.

The others nodded. They made sure to remove every trace of their being on the computer, and then shut all monitors down. Lizzie and Diego quickly pulled two chairs next to Pearl to listen in to the conversation between her and HQ. They worked on getting the connection through the device and monitors, so that the second device, which was back at HQ, could receive data and facts about the Queen's latest plans.

They were close to completing the connection process, and the only thing they had left to do was to wait until the connection was operational. Pearl decided to tell HQ about Queen Sophie's evil plans whilst they were waiting for the loading to finish.

Pearl quickly told Lizzie and Diego to keep an eye on the connection before she got into a discussion with HQ about what they had found out from the secret files. The two of them, as usual, agreed and went to check on the device. Once Lizzie and Diego were gone, Pearl picked up the Walkie-Talkie and checked in to see if anyone from HQ was still on the line.

"HQ? Anyone there? I need to report to you about the clarification time I asked for a while ago. We have found out something interesting. Please hurry up, because I don't have long until it is time for me and the others to go and complete the last phase of the mission. I will explain that too" Pearl called out, trying to reach Lora, Cooper, or Branch if they had heard her.

Someone from HQ came and picked up the Walkie-Talkie and responded to Pearl. "Okay, the tech leads are not available now, so I, one of the team members, will listen and report back to them on this conversation," the voice said.

Strangely, Pearl felt that this was not someone who was supposed to be talking to her at that moment. She had a feeling that she needed to immediately find out who she was talking to. "Hello, who am I talking to? And no games, only names!"

"Well played, princess. Just a little bit faster and you would have escaped, you know. Yes, it's me, Alexa, your Just Soc head" the now more familiar voice said.

Pearl gasped in uttermost shock "No, it can't be! How did you get to the Walkie-Talkie? It is impossible! There were always two or three people guarding it, making sure it didn't fall into the wrong hands!"

"Oh, you think that I meant all that? Ha-ha, I was just kidding! You did a great job with this plan! I mean the structure, the secrecy on point! You know, I feel like you should be the leader of the Just Soc now, instead of me!" Alexa chuckled and explained quite delightfully to Pearl what she really meant.

"So, wait, you aren't going to report us to the Queen? You are not actually working for the Queen, that's just you undercover?"

"Of course not! Nobody can stand her in all of Fantasia! But so far no one has been as brave as you to work up a conspiracy against Sophie"

"Okay, listen, I don't have much time right now. So, I have to tell you what I have just found out instead of telling the leads. Can I trust you to tell them once they are back?"

"You bet you can! Now hurry, you've got to tell me before the loading is complete, otherwise, we won't have any time left to discuss this matter!"

"Ok, great! Let me begin with our little group discussion. So, Lizzie was looking on the computer and she found some important information there. She discovered evil plans made by Queen Sophie, and believe me, they are crueler than you think they are" Pearl began, already capturing Alexa's interest.

"Go on, all attention is on you, this is making me interested!"

"Alright, we found out that the Queen is taking her cloning project to a much larger scale. She is going to make hundreds and thousands of clones so that she can use them to control all the different countries, realms, and kingdoms that are in existence! If that happens, there won't be anyone in the entire universe to be able to stop Sophie, nor will we be able to continue the Just Soc!" Pearl clarified, breaking the horrifying and surprising news to Alexa.

"You are most definitely right. We must stop this, for it could lead to some very, very bad consequences, not only for us but for every single thing we know in this world, Pearl. It is worse than you think"

"What exactly are you talking about? I really don't understand! You've got to explain if you want me to grasp your thoughts"

"What I'm trying to say, Pearl, is that with control over all of the universe, Sophie can gain power and will then be able to conquer and force everyone to do anything at her will" Alexa clarified, her voice becoming drier and hoarser by the second.

"Then she can easily take over humans, animals, and every other world of life out here! Queen Sophie would be able to defeat every obstacle in her way! The power to conquer" Pearl gasped, horrified about what she had just found out.

DOUBLE-AGENT

Pearl and Alexa had finished their little conversation just on time because Lizzie and Diego had signaled to Pearl that the transfer preparation was complete.

Lizzie came over and snatched the Walkie-Talkie from Pearl. "Okay, whoever is on the line right now, we don't have much time to talk, so start the process of transfer now. The process needs to be completed as fast as possible because the last part of this mission awaits us!" She instructed a very impressed Alexa.

"Who could have known that you had all these many talents such as leadership buried within you! That is quite truly wonderful! Of course, I'll go and start the process, the tech leads have already taught me how to do so. One second please, I will be right back!" Alexa praised her happily.

"All clear, go ahead! Once you're back, I'll explain the last phase of this mission. You must understand it very clearly" Lizzie reminded Alexa, only a few seconds before she started the process.

Pearl was puzzled. Why did Lizzie not seem confused when she heard that Alexa had been taught by Lora and Cooper how to handle the process of transfer?

"Lizzie, why are you not reacting to the fact that this person has been told how to operate the system?" Pearl asked, hoping for a clearer reply.

"Well, obviously, me and Diego listened in to your little conversation earlier and we know that you had talked to Alexa, so we aren't confused or anything about the change of voice. Now, does that explanation suit you or do I need to go into further detail?" Lizzie spoke in a very, very annoyed tone since according to her, the answer to Pearl's question was quite obvious.

"Oh ok, that makes much more sense now"

Meanwhile, Alexa had finished typing in the various codes, starting the process to transfer all the information from the secret files to a data file in HQ's data storage. "Alright, the process has started. Now, tell me, what is the last phase of our mission?" Alexa asked, returning from the room nearby, having just powered up the machinery built by the others for the mission.

"Now that we know that the Queen is playing with dangerous forces and that she must be stopped before anything goes wrong. So, we know that there is almost no way to convince Sophie to stop. That's why we've got to attack! No, it isn't what you think. We aren't going to battle her, we're only going to threaten to. Anyhow, if we did go into battle, we would lose within a matter of seconds. We have to get her to forfeit and then confess her plans, making those who still trusted Sophie lose their belief in her. Lastly, we get every citizen of Fantasia to agree to throw Queen Sophie into the dungeons once more, but this time permanently. Then, if all that happens without any problems, our mission would be completed" Lizzie recited, having practiced this explanation many times.

"That sure is clever, but I am not sure if Queen Sophie will fall for it. She is quite smart at figuring out what goes on around her, so if you do get caught, you could get into some serious trouble, and I am pretty sure you won't like it" Alexa said seriously, warning them about the possible, terrible consequences they could face because of Lizzie's plan.

"Yes, but we do need to take risks, otherwise we would never know if we could overthrow Queen Sophie by doing so" Pearl argued, trying to make a point so that Alexa would understand why Lizzie had made such a risky plan.

"Hmm…I suppose we could give it a try, if you do believe that we could get something good out of this last phase, then why should we stop? Let's do it, you just have to tell me who, what, when, where and how? Leave the rest to me" Alexa said, changing her mind and giving the plan a chance through Pearl's argument.

Lizzie, Pearl, and Diego agreed. "Okay, we'll tell you who, what, when, where, and how, and you already know why. Just give us a minute and we'll be right back" Lizzie said, before jumping out of the chair to run and tell Antonio about what they needed to do next.

Pearl peeked out the door, just to make sure that the coast was clear before they did anything. From what she saw, no one was there and so they could easily sneak out and talk to Antonio. Lizzie and Diego looked at her questioningly. Pearl nodded, and silently mouthed at them to go out and talk to Antonio so that they could explain the last phase, for which they would need his help.

Lizzie led Diego out the door on his tiptoes, trying not to make a single noise. They crept along the wall until they got close enough to Antonio for him to hear them in a very soft and silent whisper. "Psst, Antonio! Nod if you can hear me" Diego asked, seeing if they had caught Antonio's attention yet.

Antonio looked around the hallway, searching for the voice which had spoken to him. Once he noticed Diego and Lizzie standing behind some plants, he turned back and nodded, so that if anyone was watching him, they wouldn't be able to find out where Lizzie and Diego were hiding.

Diego noticed Antonio nodding. "Good. Now, it is time for the last phase, and for this, we need your help. Can I trust you to tell no one, unless you are asked to, about the information you are going to get to know?" he questioned only so they could keep this mission as secretive and secure as possible.

"You can count on me! Just tell me what I need to do, and you will have yourselves an extra sidekick" Antonio assured, seeming trustable enough to Diego and Lizzie so that they could tell him the latest updates about their mission.

Diego and Lizzie began to explain everything that happened from the moment they stepped through the door to the archive room. Antonio patiently listened to the long story, even though he started getting a bit bored by the details of the story that they were going into. After what seemed like an eternity of whispering, Diego and Lizzie had finally finished the long and far too detailed story of their time in the computer room.

"I understand what happened now, thank you, but may I ask, what help is it that you need me to do? I would like to know what it is that I will be doing before I agree to this" Antonio queried since he was quite unsure of what Lizzie, Pearl, and Diego had planned, which already made him feel scared for the upcoming events.

"We will need you to get yourself on patrol near the Queen's Throne room tomorrow morning when she declares her new cloning project. There will be five of us hiding there, ready to enter. We appear, you make an act of stumbling because of shock, which opens the door. Then the rest goes on. There will be some more people appearing at the door to the throne room, all you have to do is to lead them into the room. That's it, pretty simple, right?" Lizzie explained Antonio's part, which was safer and less scary than he thought it would be.

"Ok, it seems safe enough. You can count on me! I will be waiting for you tomorrow morning in front of the Queen's throne room!" Antonio agreed, convinced by Lizzie's simple instruction for the next day.

"Great to know! You can count on us to save Fantasia from everything!" Lizzie and Diego replied quite cheerily in chorus.

"I'd better go now, the butler is awaited. Oh, and Lizzie, you should probably slip into the staff room and change into your normal clothes. I think someone might notice that a uniform is missing if you forgot to do so" Antonio noted, before leaving the hallway to attend his duties as the Queen's butler.

"Sure! Bye, we'll meet tomorrow!" Lizzie quickly whispered after him, rather loudly.

Lizzie dragged Diego once more back to the computer room so that they could tell Pearl and Alexa what they needed to know before they cleaned up and snuck back out to rest for the day.

"Wow, that seems pretty clever to me, turning so many people against the Queen and all that! I'll make sure that everyone hears about this, they'll have to help. See you tomorrow, great champions!" Alexa said, amazed and proud at the same time, just before she switched to a different channel and turned off the Walkie-Talkie, finally done for the day.

"Ok guys let's roll! We should clean up and make this place look just like it was before we came in. Remember, it needs to be spotless so that no one is suspicious of anyone being here" Lizzie directed.

They all put the papers away, pushed in chairs, cleared the activity history of the monitors, and switched them off. The room now looked exactly like it did when they entered it a few hours ago. Lizzie looked around in complete satisfaction. They were ready to leave.

"So, Lizzie and Diego, what do you say we go and take a little rest before the next day? We've earned it, and we need to power up for tomorrow!" Pearl asked, in quite a bright mood. Lizzie and Diego nodded agreeingly.

"On the other hand, Lizzie, I think you should change back into your overalls, you definitely wouldn't want to be caught wearing that anywhere around," Pearl mentioned, eyeing the Royal Security uniform Lizzie was wearing carefully.

"Oh, thanks for telling me Pearl, imagine what would happen if I hadn't remembered at all. What are we waiting for? Time to go!" Lizzie thanked her, grateful for the little reminder. They peered through the little peephole, checking for the coast to be clear. Nobody was in sight, so they carefully stepped out and left the room.

The three of them quickly crept back to the staff room using the map they had brought so that Lizzie could slip back into her normal clothes. Once she had done so, Lizzie took the Walkie-Talkie and dialed in the channel to contact Flutter and Dwarfer. Once Flutter had heard Lizzie talking through the receiver, she immediately picked it up and started to chat.

Flutter told Lizzie about the not-so-amusing afternoon she had spent with Dwarfer downtown. In exchange, Lizzie told her briefly about their top-secret plan to overthrow Queen Sophie. Flutter was quite amazed when she heard this. She had thought that the plan was so clever that she was so shocked and amazed by it.

"Enough, enough, we need you to come over to the garden now, because we are ready to leave. You have to hurry because we can't wait for too long, we could be spotted by someone in the palace. Got to run, meet you there!" Lizzie hastily said goodbye, she needed to leave with the others to get back out to the garden.

Flutter told Dwarfer, who was keenly waiting for news from Lizzie, Pearl, and Diego, everything she had found out from them. He too, was quite awestruck when he heard what was planned for the last phase. Once Flutter had finished explaining to Dwarfer, the two of them made their way to the garden of the palace. They got into the short line for the cable car, waited for their turn, and hopped on, and once they finally reached the top, they made sure to walk around the back of the palace unnoticed.

In the meantime, Lizzie, Pearl, and Diego had made it outside to the gardens and were hiding behind the playhouse, waiting for Dwarfer and Flutter. Every few minutes, Diego peeked through the tiny window to check if they had arrived. After five or ten minutes, he saw two figures waving at him through the gate.

"Lizzie, Pearl, I see them! Let's go over! I am sure that Flutter has her magic pixie dust to remove the vines from the gate" Diego exclaimed excitedly, noticing that the two figures were Flutter and Dwarfer.

The three of them crawled out of the little, cramped playhouse and walked over to the gate. They greeted Flutter and Dwarfer, and Flutter soon began getting her pixie dust ready to use its magic so that the gates could be opened. Almost immediately after she finished sprinkling the pixie dust, the vines wrapped around the bars on the gate slid away silently like snakes.

"Nice to see you three! What a day you must have had, you deserve lots of rest and a treat!" Dwarfer exclaimed excitedly, as he warmly greeted Lizzie, Pearl, and Diego as they pushed open the gates and walked over.

"We'd love that, thanks! Let's get going before we're all spotted" Pearl answered with relief that they wouldn't need to do anything for the rest of the day.

The vines slid back into place as the gates closed. Pearl led them all down the long, sandy path around the back, stopping at the cable cars. They quickly hopped into the first one they saw. Once their car reached the bottom, Lizzie, Pearl, Diego, Flutter and Dwarfer hopped out, chatting about all sorts of things.

They walked around town for a while, checking out the shops, restaurants, and everything else the valley town had to offer. After a while, they all were tired out, and the only thing they had energy left for was a good night's sleep.

Dwarfer led them all to an empty patch of land in the forest near the valley town. Flutter seemed to have a little pixie dust left, so she pulled it out and sprinkled it all over the land. "What are you doing?" Lizzie asked curiously.

"I figured I could magically make a cabin for the night since we're all so tired. I know that no one wants to sleep on mud, because I don't want to, that's for sure" Flutter explained.

"Not at all! I'd rather sleep in a comfortable cabin if that's what you're making" Diego said, agreeing with Flutter.

Suddenly, there was a loud bang. Tree logs and wooden planks started to appear out of nowhere, and they started to move together as if they were building a puzzle. At last, after a few minutes of waiting, all the pieces had been put into place, forming a log cabin, just like the ones they had rented the night before.

"That's awesome! Show us inside, Flutter!" Diego excitedly jumped around.

"Sure, why not! Come on everyone! We'll get a good night's sleep in here!" Flutter said, trying to seem encouraging.

Flutter stepped up to the brown, wooden door and turned the doorknob, revealing a bright and colorful room, with plenty of cushions and sofas for all of them.

"Wow! You aren't pretending at all! This place is great, Flutter!" I'm going inside first!" Diego said in amazement, looking at the brilliant cabin room with the eyes of a child.

They all followed a giggling Diego inside. The interior was even more impressive than they had expected! The ceiling was high above them, with a beautiful glass chandelier hanging from above. There was a magnificently large snack bar in the right corner, and the food there was just like the tasty meals Damien cooked back at the inn.

Dwarfer's eyes widened once he spotted the gigantic snack bar. "This is going to be an enjoyable night, folks! Especially with all this delicious food..." he excitedly announced, rubbing his hands, as if he were getting ready for an important race.

Meanwhile, Pearl had found herself a large basket of wool and knitting needles and was knitting like crazy. She had already knitted half a blanket. Everyone stared at Pearl as she quickly knitted row by row. After a while, Pearl noticed that everyone was looking at her. "What? I used to love knitting when I was younger, but now that I am the Mermaid Princess, I never have the time to. Let's just say that I am a bit of a professional when it comes to knitting" she said in annoyance. The others immediately stopped staring. Pearl smiled back at everyone as they continued to explore the beautiful cabin room.

Diego was jumping around on soft cushions and sofas, Dwarfer was munching his way through the entire snack bar, Pearl was continuing to knit her Rapunzel on a blanket and Flutter was gathering more pixie dust. Lizzie was the only one who hadn't yet found anything to do. As she strolled around the large room, she stumbled upon a small table with a single drawer. Lizzie bent down and pulled the little drawer open. She found nothing in the drawer, but she still wasn't completely sure she had searched everywhere in that drawer.

Lizzie thought that there might be a false bottom. She pressed down on the drawer, and sure enough, the real bottom of the drawer sprung open. Lizzie picked up a thick, brown book from inside. The title, "The Beautiful Magic of Fantasia" was written in big, bold letters on the cover. Lizzie blew away the greyish dust on the book and opened it because she was far too curious to resist the temptation to do so.

Inside the book, there were pages and pages of information about all the magical things in Fantasia, which Lizzie had already seen with her own two eyes. "What use is this book to me if I know more than this says in the first place?" Lizzie sighed, flipping to the end of the book. As she was about to close it, the book suddenly began to glow quite brightly. Seconds later, it magically floated into the air, glowing even brighter than before. Then the book started spinning, faster and faster by the second

As all this happened, Lizzie just stared, almost as still as a statue. Soon the book was spinning around so fast, it had caught everyone's attention in the room. Diego, Dwarfer, Pearl and Flutter were all gaping at the book and Lizzie, as a strong, glittering tornado swirled around her.

Flutter was the first one to come to her senses. She ran forward and leaped, pushing Lizzie to the ground, away from the monstrous tornado. "Ow, Flutter, what was that for!" Lizzie complained, rubbing the spot on her arm which had hit the hard ground.

"I was saving you from who knows what! Something bad could have happened, especially since there's magic in it!" Flutter argued defensively.

However, just then, something strange happened. The book stopped spinning and fell to the ground with a thud. It was no longer glowing brightly, however, it did have a little sparkle to it. Everyone thought it was just a little mistake in the magic pixie spell Flutter had conducted and went back to what they were doing before the strange event. All of a sudden, a bright glow of light burst out of the open pages of the book. It was far too much for the five of them to watch, so they all looked away from the golden, shining rays.

"What is happening here! Flutter! You have to fix this, I can't do this much longer! UGH!" Lizzie groaned, straining to see in the blinding brightness.

Flutter couldn't take it any longer. "I DON'T HAVE A CLUE ABOUT ANYTHING THAT'S GOING ON NOW! DON'T ALWAYS EXPECT FOR ME TO HAVE THE ANSWER WHEN IT COMES TO MY MAGIC! I'M NOT AN ENCYCLOPEDIA ABOUT PIXIE MAGIC!" Flutter roared angrily at Lizzie, squinting the tears away as she raged furiously.

Lizzie was quite shocked and offended by that. She slumped her shoulders, her curious, adventure-seeking expression falling to a saddened appearance. It seemed like she was about to burst into tears, but Lizzie was trying to stop them from coming.

By then, Flutter had calmed down and was thinking about what she had said to Lizzie earlier. She realized what she had done. "Oh no! I let my emotions get the better of me! I am a Pixie, and I will not be rude or harmful! I must apologize to poor Lizzie, what she must be feeling because of my emotions!" Flutter thought regretfully. However, before Flutter had a chance to make things better, an unknown person stepped out of the bright light and went over to Lizzie, wrapping her in a warm bear hug.

Lizzie suddenly smelled a whirl of light and airy scents around her. She sniffed carefully, feeling something that was familiar with but unsure what it was. Just then, she sensed someone behind her. She had no idea who it was, so she turned around to see. Recognizing the familiar face, Lizzie froze, in utter shock.

TRUTHS

"Gran!?! H...h...how are you here? You shouldn't be alive!" Lizzie stammered, puzzled that of all people, her lovely Gran was standing in front of her.

"It's lovely to see you, my sunshine. My oh my, how much you've grown! These must be your lovely friends, Dwarfer, Diego, Princess Pearl, and Flutter, am I right? Wonderful to see you all in person! You must be wondering about how I even got here in the first place. It's a long story, to be honest. Let me explain everything over a nice cup of my tea, I see that you're all quite exhausted" Betty replied, comforting Lizzie while she heard the soft, velvety tone of her Gran's voice.

They all sat down on the couch, watching Betty make the tea in the little kettle they had. Once everyone was settled, each with a cup of tea and a few biscuits, Betty began to tell them the story of how she ended up there from the book.

"It all began when Marcus was no longer King. I was very loyal to him, as you all should know and would never give him or his plans away. I fought to keep the Fantasian tradition alive, letting go of my own wonderfully happy life with everything I loved end forever so that no harm would be done to you, Lizzie. You were my most precious treasure and I couldn't bear to lose you ever, so I sacrificed myself for you. Sophie accepted the deal I proposed and so I let myself be trapped in the pages of this book for the rest of my life" Betty explained, tears welling up in her eyes and expression saddening as she recalled the last few events of her past life in Fantasia.

"But Gran, if you were trapped in there forever, how did you escape today? You surely can't break a pixie's spell on your own" Lizzie asked curiously.

"I believe you would understand better if a pixie explained this to you. Flutter, will you?" Betty said, still sniffling a little.

"We pixies are taught this secret at a very young age. I'm only telling you because it is really important. So, when a pixie or pixie magic casts a powerful spell involving humans or any living things, those creatures can't break it themselves, unless they have their magic equal nearby. If their equal is nearby, it will break the spell and let the creature free. It is the creature's choice if they want to escape or not, but in Mrs. Thomas's case, she decided to leave. The book she was trapped in ended up here randomly, I don't know how. That's pretty much it" Flutter told them.

"Well... Who was the magic equal to Mrs. Thomas?" Diego questioned.

"First of all, please do call me Betty! It makes me feel too old when you call me Mrs. Thomas. I assume that would be Lizzie since she was the first one who came across the book. She gets her magic from me" Betty exclaimed, winking playfully.

"That does make sense Betty, no one else saw or touched the book before Lizzie! Now that we've fixed that matter, there's a lot of catching up to be done. Let me start!" Pearl excitedly announced, volunteering before anyone else could say anything.

"Um... I don't know how to say this to you Princess, but if you don't mind, I'd like to spend the rest of the time before we go to bed, with Lizzie, alone. Have a good night's sleep!" Betty awkwardly interrupted, dragging Lizzie outside through the back door of the wondrous cabin and into the clear, starry night.

"Gran, remember once how you and I went down to the hills on the farm and watched the beautiful stars? You showed me the constellations, I remember our favorite ones being the Big Dipper and the Little Dipper! I forgot why though. Do you remember, Gran?" Lizzie mentioned, looking back at her enjoyable memories with her Gran.

"Yes, we both loved those constellations, because they represented you and me and how much we loved each other. Betty Dipper, Lizzie Dipper, that's what you called them. You were so adorable back then!" Betty recalled, sighing happily.

"Anyways, Lizzie dear, I see that you're wearing that amulet I gave you. It's very precious to me, you know, there's a whole family history behind it. I think it's time you knew the whole story behind the reason you're here with me in the first place" she added.

"I always thought it was just because of the amulet. I never would have known that there was more of a backstory"

THE MAGIC OF THE AMULET

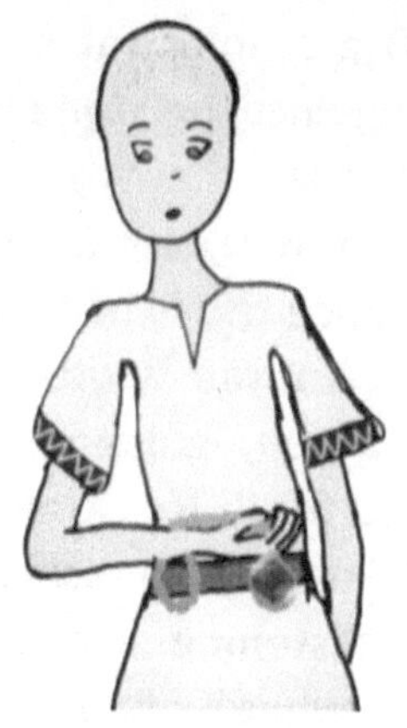

A long time ago, in the high mountains of Scotland, a magical jewel was created. It was very powerful, and it could be dangerous if it fell into the wrong hands. One day, an adventurous scholar was venturing into the high peaks to collect precious medicine for his sick teacher. As it started to rain heavily, the scholar started to search for a cave to take shelter in. After hours of searching, he came across a large opening. Assuming it was just a normal cave, he walked in, not knowing the amazing discovery he would make.

The scholar sat down in a corner, leaning his head against the stone wall. Suddenly, a bright light shone over the whole cave. The scholar turned away from it, afraid of what he would be faced with. Once the light faded away, the scholar turned around to see a little red box, gloriously sitting upon a tall, golden pillar. The scholar curiously reached for it. He carefully opened the lid, revealing a truly magical treasure inside. It was a shiny, red ruby, glistening like a star. The scholar couldn't believe what he had found. He knew that he had to get it back to his teacher, Master Zin, for he would surely know what to do with the strangely pretty jewel.

Forgetting about the medicine he was supposed to find for his master, the scholar ran down the mountain paths in the hard, wet rain. He held the box containing the precious jewel he had found tightly as he ran. Once the scholar had finally reached the little hut in the village where his master lived, he immediately began to tell him the whole tale, pulling out the magical ruby he had found.

Master Zin recognized the precious jewel in an instant. The Ancient jewel of Myths. This jewel would give people ultimate powers from any myth or legend, but only if they believed in it. The scholar, amazed by the small yet impressive jewel, asked his Master about what they would do with it. Master Zin insisted that his scholar keep the jewel. When the scholar asked why, Master Zin told him that he just knew that the jewel would be in safe hands with his trustworthy scholar.

Many years later, the wise scholar of Master Zin had made himself a beautiful family and was a happy grandfather to a wonderful girl. He had made a gold-chained amulet to keep the precious red ruby safe. He and his granddaughter also shared a truly remarkable interest in the fantastic tales of the world, especially the legend of Fantasia, the favorite of his granddaughter.

Its power was the strongest of the jewel could grant, however also the most dangerous. With the belief of that legend, the ancient jewel can grant you the ability to become part of any of the many environments in Fantasia. There was only one person the Scholar knew who could take control of the strong and magical powers of the amulet's red ruby. As he watched his granddaughter reading the books of myths and legends, he had given her, he knew where the amulet and its jewel truly belonged.

* * *

“Gran, how can this fit with what you told me before? Didn’t your grandfather find the ruby?” Lizzie asked, somewhat confused by the tale.

“Put it all together, dear. You should be able to understand then”

“Hmmm… Wait, you’re saying that this scholar is your GRANDFATHER? That is just… amazing!”

“Indeed. He passed this amulet onto me and now it belongs to you. I’m sure that in the future, you will give this to your most trusted and loved one and so on. It was about time anyway, for you to understand the true history of your present”

“If you don’t mind, Gran, could you tell me who Master Zin is? No one I know is called Zin”

Lizzie’s Gran tried to recall any memory of her grandfather telling her about Master Zin, only to remember nothing at all. She shook her head disappointedly, telling Lizzie that she too didn’t know who Master Zin was and couldn’t remember any information which possibly could be about him.

“That’s something we both should probably figure out together, right Gran?” Lizzie noted, trying to lift the silent mood.

“Agreed. Now, let’s talk about this big barge in action you’re doing tomorrow. Anything I should do?” Betty asked, changing the subject.

"Before I say anything else, how do YOU know that we planned all this?"

"Let's just say that the magical object I was trapped in was somehow following you and I could hear you guys from the book I was in"

"Turns out that we have a whole lot of things to learn about pixie magic. It seems so powerful!"

"Of course! We could ask Flutter to tell us more!"

"Back to our barge-in action. There is one way you can help, Gran. We will need..."

A FAMILIAR DREAM

"... you to gather a rebellion outside of the palace. Tell everyone to tell their friends and family working at the palace to join too! That way the Queen will be almost defenseless! Can you do that? People will listen to you" Lizzie quietly whispered, explaining the favor she needed.

"My, don't you have big plans! They seem awesome too! But Lizzie, darling, are you sure that you need this?" her Gran asked doubtfully, just to make sure that she wouldn't be doing anything unnecessarily.

"Yes, Gran! Otherwise, the Queen's defense will be too strong for us and she will take victory away from us like child's play! You know that we can't let that happen at any cost, all of Fantasia is relying on us!"

Betty was taken aback at her granddaughter's fierceness and independence. She smiled, remembering her young self, a replica of Lizzie. "Calm down, dear. I was just checking to be sure. I will definitely be there at the palace tomorrow, with the best and biggest rebellion you would have ever seen in your life. Pinkie-Promise!" Betty promised.

"Thanks Gran, you're the best! I knew I could count on you!" Lizzie thanked her, wrapping her Gran into a big, warm hug.

"I'm your Gran, Lizzie! Who else would I do so much for, other than you and Annie?" Betty said, happily hugging her back.

"Anyway, I'm tired, I'll be heading to bed now"

"Yes, go to bed now. In the meantime, I will start to assemble the people, because trust me, making a rebellion of the size you're asking for, is not easy at all. Tell the others, will you? Good Night Lizzie!"

"Good Night Gran! Stay safe!" Lizzie shouted after her Gran, as she walked away to the nearby town.

Lizzie stayed outside for a while, cherishing her memories with her family and friends whom she missed, every minute of her days in Fantasia. "At least Gran is here with me. That's what matters right now. That and saving Fantasia from the reign of Queen Sophie" she thought, trying to feel less homesick.

Just about then, Pearl appeared through the doorway, telling Lizzie to go to bed. She sighed, turning away from the beautiful night skies to go inside. As Lizzie passed her, Pearl sensed that something was up with Lizzie. She walked up to Lizzie and asked "Lizzie, you seem a bit down. What's up?".

“I miss… everything! I mean I love Fantasia and all, but I feel like… I just want to be back at the farm, living my old life with Mum, Dad, Annie and Gran! I… can’t take this anymore” Lizzie wailed, feeling more homesick than she had ever been in her entire journey through Fantasia.

“You know, wherever you may be in the world, there is only one place that you can truly call home. You may not know it, but me, Diego, Dwarfer, and Flutter are homesick all the time, but we do know that missing our homes for a while is worth it, if in the end, we’ll all be even happier. It isn’t so bad when you think of it this way” Pearl said, trying to comfort Lizzie.

Lizzie, who was still in a dull mood, had heard what Pearl had told her, and had realized that she had left everything she loved, for a much bigger reason. “You know what, I think that I’ll forget about being homesick right now. There are far more important things to think about now” she said as the two of them walked to the beds hat had magically appeared whilst Lizzie and her Gran were outside, thanks to Flutter’s pixie dust spells. Pearl just nodded, relieved that Lizzie had calmed down once again.

Everyone got into their beds, and not surprisingly fell asleep quickly, to rest their tired muscles after the long day they had. They all dreamed about wonderful things, like riding rainbows or being at an all-you-can-eat buffet. However, Lizzie dreamed of something she had undoubtedly dreamed of before.

Lizzie stood in the middle of a room that looked somewhat like the throne room of Queen Sophie's palace. There was a short dwarf, a young boy, a glittery green pixie, and a beautiful princess with a glamorous tiara accompanying her. Each of them held different items. A little bag of pixie dust, a slingshot, a satchel, a trident, and Lizzie's amulet were the so-called weapons they all had.

There were also other people in the throne room other than them. Mermaids, dwarves, giants, pixies, and talking trees were all gathered in the hall, whispering and murmuring as they watched Lizzie and those who accompanied her. Lizzie stood face to face with someone who looked like the Queen, or as Lizzie imagined, the Queen herself.

"That jewel will be mine, and I will soon rule all the realms in the world! Hahahahahahahaha!" Sophie announced, cackling so loudly that its echo rang in everyone's ears throughout the room.

Lizzie tossed and turned uncomfortably, unable to fall asleep. She kept hearing the Queen's cold voice in her head, over and over again. It kept saying different phrases each time and, Lizzie could barely understand what they were supposed to mean.

"Why can't I just sleep? At least leave me alone!" Lizzie thought, far too tired to do anything more.

All of a sudden, the Queen's voice began to speak in Lizzie's head. It whispered, "You... will... not... use... those... powers!".

Lizzie kept hearing that same phrase again and again. She once more tried to understand what it was supposed to mean, only failing. Looking back at the time she had spent with her Gran earlier that night, Lizzie suddenly understood. She abruptly sat up, panting heavily. Pearl heard Lizzie and almost immediately got up. Lizzie, noticing Pearl motioned for her to come over.

"She... knows..." Lizzie said out of breath, collapsing onto the ground immediately after.

THE ASSOCIATION OF ANCIENT ALLIES

Lizzie blinked. She saw Flutter and Pearl kneeling in front of her, looking quite desperate and worried. As soon as Pearl noticed that Lizzie was awake, the scared expression on her face disappeared. "Oh, Lizzie! I was so worried that you were badly hurt! I am so glad!" Pearl exclaimed, relieved that nothing terrible had happened.

"Yes, yes. But Sophie knows! She knows that I have the amulet and she wants it really badly" Lizzie reminded her, still very panicked.

Flutter sensed that this was important. She didn't understand what Lizzie meant, so she tried to calm her down so she could explain to them. "Lizzie, take a few deep breaths and then explain. We can't help you if we don't know what's going on" she said.

Lizzie did exactly that, telling Flutter and Pearl, and eventually, Diego and Dwarfer, who had been woken up by all the commotion in the room about the story her Gran had told her earlier. After that, she told everyone about her strange dreams and about the most recent one she had. Lizzie told them about the people, especially Queen Sophie and the puzzling phrases.

"In the end, I was able to understand the last phrase in tonight's dream. The amulet has special powers, as you already know, and I am pretty sure that Sophie has known about it for a long time. This must mean that she knows about... us! Everything fits, except I don't understand why she would just let us get this far without throwing every one of us into the dungeons" Lizzie finished.

"Maybe she wanted to wait for the right moment to seize the amulet and take over the world? I mean, she couldn't just capture us like that" Flutter suggested, still as unsure as the others.

"That's it! The missing piece to the puzzle! It all makes sense now! Flutter is right, Sophie did want to wait for the right time to take over, because she didn't want to be too obvious!" Diego explained excitedly.

"How'd you figure that out? What are the pieces of the puzzle, Diego? You're definitely onto something" Dwarfer asked curiously.

"I think that Pearl should tell you all a story, to help you understand what I'm talking about. I know that she knows it much better than I do" Diego told them, looking at Pearl, who just shrugged and nodded at him.

"Aright, I'll tell, but you all have to promise me that you won't tell anyone at all, please?" Pearl said, making sure that everyone had agreed.

"Lizzie, your red ruby is something more important than just the Ancient jewel of Myths. There is even more to it than you think and I'm pretty sure that this will be helpful for you, Lizzie" Pearl began.

Lizzie was amazed by how much there was to know about her amulet. "That sounds interesting! I would have never found out any of this without you guys! Thank you so much!" Lizzie told them thankfully.

THE ASSOCIATION OF ANCIENT ALLIES

Over hundreds and thousands of years ago, five magical jewels were formed, to protect all dimensions in the world from evil hands. The diamond had the power to bring anything said by its user to life, the emerald had the ability to combine facts and data to create knowledgeable and strong powers temporarily, the jade controlled the forces created by the best and most intriguing literature, and the amber could recreate dreams. However, the most powerful jewel of them all was the red ruby.

When all these jewels are brought together, they create an ultimate strength that can defeat anything. Also, together they can enhance all five powers, giving each power a boost to strengthen it. All five jewels are contained within a piece of jewelry such as an amulet or a bracelet, created by its owner.

The combined power of all these jewels is even more dangerous in the wrong hands than the red ruby alone. If these strong powers are used in the wrong way, they could end up harming all dimensions.

Each holder of a jewel is part of the Association of Ancient allies. They are an unstoppable force of good, who stop evil by all means necessary. Currently, there is no trace of this association anywhere in the universe. Those who are chosen to be jewel holders are the only ones who can control the magic forces of the jewels safely.

* * *

"Pearl, but... why didn't you tell us about all this! We would have been much further ahead if we had known! You knew all along!" Lizzie exclaimed angrily.

Pearl sighed. "It wasn't exactly easy for me either, you know. I was staying in the palace once with my mother and grandmother. I had just finished playing a round of hide-and-seek and I was very tired. When I walked into the suite we were in, I saw a strange book on the table. It had an interesting symbol on it, one that I had never seen. So to satisfy my curiosity, I walked over to it and started to read. That was when I found out about the jewels. I marveled at the beautiful images of them in awe. Just as I was about to turn to the next page, I heard my mother leading my grandmother into the room" Pearl started.

"What happened next, Pearl? We all want to know!" Diego asked her curiously.

"Well, I had to run and hide inside a nearby cupboard, so they didn't see me. They came in and sat on the couch and my mother took the book. That's when I found out about the association of Ancient allies. My grandmother was very worried. She and my mother talked about the association and how they had all disappeared. Also, I learned that the ruby was lost somewhere. My grandmother mentioned the jade jewel and showed it to my mother. Then she said that I would be the one to use the power of the jewel in the future. And that's where I jumped out of the closet and ran over to my grandmother. That was when I had to promise that I would never tell anyone about it, because if someone knew about everything, the jewels and our secret society they could become greedy, destroying the association and its remains" Pearl finished.

"If you were supposed to have the jewel in the future, where is it? I mean, I can't see any jewel on you" Flutter pointed out.

"I hid it because I knew that if Queen Sophie saw the jade jewel at all, she'd demand I give it to her. I'm wearing it in my charm necklace, not the Pearl one" Pearl explained.

"I don't see it in your necklace, Pearl. Did you put it in some secret portal, or does it not even exist?" Lizzie asked jokingly.

“Of course it does! Look, I have an opening here and if you press two times on the photo of my grandmother, it will open up and show the jade jewel. Try it!” Pearl told them.

Lizzie pressed twice on the photo of Pearl’s grandmother and to her surprise, it did reveal the jade jewel. Everyone was intrigued by the shiny blue stone, glittering in the bright light of the room. For a while, everyone was admiring the beautiful jade without distractions. However, soon the five of them became bored. They all sat in silence until Lizzie interrupted the peace with a question.

“What happened to the other allies?” Lizzie questioned.

Pearl seemed quite troubled by Lizzie’s question; everybody could tell. Pearl stuttered, “T…the… other… allies?”.

THE ALLIES' PAST

The others sensed that something wasn't right. Pearl had walked outside on her own, leaving Lizzie, Flutter, Diego, and Dwarfer inside. She didn't even respond to Lizzie's question before going into the garden.

Lizzie nodded to the others and went out into the garden. Once again, she was overwhelmed by the beautiful skies around her. Pearl was sitting down on the soft, green grass and gazing into the wonderful landscape in front of them. Lizzie joined her and for a while, they both admired the night around them.

All of a sudden, Pearl burst into tears. "It's all my fault! I shouldn't have..." she wailed, waking Lizzie with a jolt.

Lizzie was puzzled. Did Pearl have something to do with the disappearance of the other members of the association? Pearl was acting pretty weird earlier, and she didn't even try to predict what had happened to the other allies! "That isn't like her!" Lizzie thought.

"Pearl, look, I can't help unless you tell me what's going on. So, take a few breaths and then talk to me, ok?" Lizzie told Pearl, calming the situation.

“Ok. I’m sorry I didn’t tell you guys earlier, but I am the reason that Queen Sophie was able to capture the other allies. We were all trying to stop her from taking down Fantasia’s most valued place: The Museum. One minute we were about to defeat her, and the next she had us all in a trap”

“Okay, so what happened next?”

“She had your Gran captured by one of her supporters and I forgot that my power was being used to protect the rest of us. I let go and tried to fight back at the Queen, but I failed and when I searched for the others, they were gone, along with Betty” she finished.

Lizzie was stunned. She had so many things she wanted to ask Pearl, but she figured that it could wait until she had taken in everything. The both of them sat there in silence and were eventually joined by the others. None of them uttered a single word for a while, so they all enjoyed the lovely silence.

After some time, Dwarfer had become bored by the peace and quiet, so he decided to interrupt it by asking Pearl a question.

“Pearl, we heard your conversation earlier and we understand, if one of us saw our loved ones being captured, we would probably forget about everything else. Also, I want to ask you something” he said, trying to show some empathy for Pearl.

Flutter and Diego smiled at Dwarfer, happy that he was for once taking action on his own. However, Lizzie was the complete opposite. She glared at him like she was about to explode with anger.

Pearl, however, did notice Lizzie's expression and whispered to her, "It's fine, Lizzie. No need to get so worked up over something so small, really!". Lizzie took a few breaths and agreed, leaving Pearl to talk to Dwarfer.

"Thanks for understanding. Now, what is it that you want to know?" Pearl asked him.

"I wanted to ask if you know where the other allies were trapped because we might be able to rescue them once we defeat the Queen. I'm sure it's worth a try!" Dwarfer explained.

"I know that Queen Sophie took them into her palace... but where in the palace?" Pearl recalled.

Suddenly, they heard a voice behind them. "The dungeons, Pearl! Where else would Sophie put James, Talia, and Daniel" it exclaimed.

They all turned around. "Betty!" Flutter and Diego shrieked in unison. The two of them got up and walked over immediately and were soon joined by Lizzie, Pearl, and Dwarfer. All five of them made sure that Betty was caught up, especially Lizzie. Everyone had to calm her down a few times because she was far too excited to stay calm!

In the middle of their conversation, Pearl's thoughts wandered back to what Betty had said earlier. Slowly she began to understand it all. It all clicked into one place. Pearl had to tell Lizzie. She pulled Lizzie over to one side. Lizzie was quite confused. Pearl only told her to be inside in a few minutes, before pushing her back to the others and heading inside.

Lizzie could tell by the focused expression on Pearl's face that it was important. She hastily thanked her Gran for the help and hurried inside. Pearl was pacing back and forth, deep in her thoughts. Once she spotted Lizzie though, she stopped pacing and sat down. Lizzie pulled up a beanbag and joined her.

Pearl explained "I know how to rescue the other allies from the dungeons!! You see, the only way they could escape would be by using their jewels. I'm 100 percent positive that Sophie took away their jewels, leaving them hopeless to escape. If we retrieve the jewels from Sophie, we could go down to the dungeons and return them to the rightful owners and then they can free themselves by using their powers!".

"That sounds good to me, Pearl. But remember, we will have to leave the others behind since they don't have anything to protect them. It is far too dangerous!" Lizzie reminded her. Pearl nodded in agreement. She too knew the dangers of bringing Flutter, Diego, and Dwarfer with them to rescue the allies.

"Now that we've settled that, can you do me a favor by telling me about the other allies? It would help to know" Lizzie requested.

"Sure! I'll start with Talia. She is the holder of the diamond jewel and is mostly quiet until it comes to using her powers. Daniel is the holder of the emerald jewel and he is the brains of the group, kind of like Diego, and lastly, James. He is the holder of the amber jewel, and also Talia's best friend. All of them are great people, and it would be great for you to meet them!" Pearl said.

"I would love to get to know them, but right now we don't have time for that. We need to stop Queen Sophie!" Lizzie mentioned.

"You're right, Lizzie. We need to focus on stopping her, to save all of Fantasia!" Pearl agreed.

By then Betty, Diego, Flutter, and Dwarfer were back inside. Pearl and Lizzie then explained in detail their plan to rescue the other allies. Betty agreed with them instantly and the others agreed as well, after a bit of an argument. "It's good that Dwarfer asked me about the other allies, otherwise we would never have figured out how to rescue them. Cheers to Dwarfer!" Pearl exclaimed.

"Cheers!" Lizzie, Betty, Diego, and Flutter responded in chorus.

Everybody relaxed for a while, enjoying themselves properly, which was something, they hadn't done in a while. They played games, had delicious food, and told each other funny stories. By the time it was dawn, they were still laughing!

Luckily, Lizzie noticed and alerted Pearl. They both stood up. "It's time to save Fantasia and restore justice! Lizzie, let's go!" Pearl announced proudly.

A WHOLE NEW WORLD

Pearl took her bracelet and chanted a few strange words. Once she said them, an exquisite jade blue suit appeared, covered in hard, teal-colored shiny scales and fins, accompanied by a glittering golden tiara with the jade jewel placed in the middle. Lizzie was amazed by how different Pearl looked in her new ally outfit. "Well, what are you waiting for? Just say, 'Antiqua magicae virtute' and you'll be transformed too!" Pearl explained.

Lizzie shrugged. She held up her amulet and chanted "Antiqua magicae virtute!". To her surprise, a few seconds later, a beautiful ruby red suit coated in waves of soft silk, appeared along with a tall staff, in which the red ruby was placed. Lizzie's Gran walked over to Lizzie and hugged her proudly.

"The first time I transformed, my grandfather was so happy and told me, in the future when I saw my children transform, it would feel the same. He was right. Today it feels so wonderful to see you take my place Lizzie, and I'm sure it will be like that for everyone in the future. Now, go out there and make me proud!" her Gran told her.

Lizzie nodded. She felt as ready as ever, to act her part as one of the allies, to end the reign of all evil, and to let justice prevail everywhere. Pearl grabbed her by the hand, and all of a sudden, they were in the air, flying further and further away from the little cabin standing alone in the dawn. Lizzie marveled over the awakening valley and the majestic palace as they soared above. She wondered if she would ever be able to do such amazing things as Pearl could. Lizzie looked at Pearl and sighed disappointedly. Pearl looked back and saw the lack of confidence in Lizzie.

"Don't be like that, Lizzie. It will come to you when the time is right. Right now we have other things to worry about, alright?" Pearl told her.

Lizzie just nodded blankly. She still wasn't convinced by Pearl, after all, Pearl already had her awesome powers and ideas, but Lizzie knew that they had no time, and she had no choice but to believe her. A few minutes later, they landed on the rooftops of the Queen's palace. Pearl let go of Lizzie's hand and suggested, "Maybe you can give it a try now?".

"No, I don't want to. I'm not feeling the connection anyway. Even if I do try, I know it won't work, and we'd just be wasting time" Lizzie refused.

"Don't be so demotivating! But, if you don't want to, that's ok. You'll be ready for it eventually, Lizzie" Pearl told her.

Pearl once again grabbed Lizzie's hand, and the next moment, they were standing inside Queen Sophie's bedroom in the palace. Pearl began to search through the whole room. Lizzie was confused. "Pearl! What on earth are you doing! Why are you searching through Sophie's bedroom?" she whisper-shouted.

"I know that the other jewels are in here, trust me! I just need to find them!"

"If you say so, Pearl. But I don't think that someone like Queen Sophie would put anything important in obvious places"

"Yeah, you're right. We should probably look closer"

Pearl and Lizzie searched in drawers, cupboards, boxes, and even bags, but they weren't successful at all. After a while, they were frustrated, and they had given up. Pearl and Lizzie lay on Queen Sophie's bed, disappointed.

"You know, Lizzie, what I don't understand is that we've searched everywhere, and we still can't find the jewels. I mean, I used my powers to find out where the jewels were, and it said it was in here. Powers are never wrong!" Pearl said, irritated.

Just then something came to Lizzie's mind. "Pearl, where did we find the password to the computers?" she questioned.

"Um... in a drawer with a false bottom?"

"Yes, so don't you think that we should be looking for something of the sort? The diamond, emerald, and amber jewels need to be hidden well as they can't easily blend in with any other jewelry, so Queen Sophie probably did exactly that!"

"Of course! You know Lizzie, you're doing great, even without any powers!" Pearl told her proudly.

The both of them went back to searching in all the places they had checked before. As Lizzie walked over to the nightstand, she stumbled and crashed into the wall. Pearl noticed that Lizzie had fallen onto the ground. She quickly ran and helped her up.

"Are you alright? There are lots of things lying around here, we've got to watch out for them. I hope it's nothing bad!" Pearl asked worriedly.

Lizzie dusted herself off and assured, "I'm fine, the suit protected my fall anyhow. No need to be worried!".

"Good to know! Anyways, have you found anything yet? I can't seem to find false bottoms or hidden slots anywhere!" Pearl told.

Lizzie looked over to the wall and noticed a strange button poking out of it. "Maybe we should try that?" she suggested, pointing towards the button she had just noticed up on the wall.

“I’ve never seen something like this before! Quick! Press It! Maybe this is where Queen Sophie has hidden the jewels!”

Lizzie pressed the button, revealing an entirely new room. And there, on a table in the middle of the room, were the three missing jewels. Pearl, and Lizzie couldn’t believe it. They had finally found the jewels – and a secret room!

“I can’t believe it, Pearl! We found the jewels and even more! I’m wondering what more the Queen has hidden in here...” Lizzie exclaimed enthusiastically, picking up the jewels and pocketing them.

“Well... Sophie wouldn’t hide anything in a room that’s already secret. I’m sure there’s something about the allies in here because this room is the only place in the palace where the Queen could have any secrets” Pearl noted, looking over to an open cabinet.

Lizzie saw the open cabinet. She walked over and stood on her tiptoes, peering inside. There was an overfilled file, with lots of papers falling out. Lizzie gathered the papers that were strewn all over the cabinet and carefully pulled out the file. “I believe that this is what we’re looking for” Lizzie announced, holding up the file triumphantly.

SECRETS

Lizzie set the heavy file down on the table. Together she and Pearl looked through the piles of papers inside it. Most of the things were just useless contracts and other things, but one section of papers particularly caught their attention. Pearl had noticed the symbol of the association on one of the papers, so they put it aside to read later, continuing to search through the overfilled file.

The two of them finished looking through the file, disappointed to have found only one small set of papers. Pearl sighed and said, "We might as well read what we've got here". Lizzie nodded and picked up the little stack. She then began to read the first page. The Queen had gathered detailed information about the association, some of which not even Pearl had known. However, this only bored both of them and Lizzie continued to read the next few pages, only to feel she was waste time.

"Pearl, can I stop reading this? It's getting boring, and I doubt that we'll find anything of use" Lizzie asked, hoping that Pearl would be reasonable.

“No, we should read everything, because who knows, something important might show up, even though it is quite boring. We most definitely cannot miss such opportunities” Pearl told her, disagreeing completely, much to Lizzie’s disappointment.

Lizzie sighed and continued to read in boredom. A few pages later, they found something interesting. It was a little note written on the printed-out page by Queen Sophie herself. “The only thing that can protect jewels is when they are close to their holders. Otherwise, they can change and not in a good way” Lizzie read.

Her eyes widened. Lizzie had just understood something important. “Pearl, do you know what this means? Talia, Daniel, and James are here! If they weren't here somewhere, Queen Sophie wouldn’t be able to use the jewels at all!” she explained excitedly.

Pearl listened carefully to her, in complete agreement. Lizzie didn’t need powers to be a great person. In Pearl’s view, Lizzie was an enthusiastic, adventure-craving girl and smart. “Lizzie, we need to find them if they are in here! Without them, we won’t have a chance of defeating the Queen!” Pearl recalled, regaining focus on their mission.

Lizzie nodded in agreement. Pearl and Lizzie started to search the room for someplace the Queen could have hidden Talia, Daniel, and James. Pearl was looking under the table when she noticed a small trapdoor on the floor. She motioned for Lizzie to come over and together they opened the trapdoor. They both climbed down the ladder and into a dark, gloomy room.

In the room, there wasn't anything other than a few chains and shackles, rags, and three prisoners. Pearl conjured some fire, to see better in the dark room. A few seconds later, Pearl shrieked, quite relieved "Talia! Daniel! James! I've found you!" recognizing who the prisoners in the room were.

A tired, weak voice spoke quietly in response. "Pearl, Betty, you've come to rescue... us..." it said, trailing off into the distance.

"Not quite, you did get two things wrong. We kind of need your help for something very urgently and I'm not Betty" Lizzie corrected.

"Then who are you? Talia thought so because you look almost exactly like Betty in your suit. You must be related to her somehow!" another voice called out loudly, but still quite weary and faint.

"I'm Elizabeth Thomas, the granddaughter of Elizabeth or 'Betty' Thomas. You can all call me Lizzie" Lizzie introduced.

"Good to know, Lizzie! I'm sure we all have many other questions, but those can wait. The important question is, what urgent help do you need? You'd better hurry because soon the Queen will come down to check on us" a third voice said, trying to sound more enthusiastic, but clearly far too exhausted.

"We need you to transform, we've got each of your jewels and help us defeat the Queen. Lizzie has a clever plan, so don't even try to argue. Only all of our powers together will work, so we hope you see how important it is" Pearl explained before Lizzie had the chance to say anything at all.

"You have our jewels! And you want us to transform too! That is amazing! By the way, I'm James, the holder of the amber jewel. But don't you know how dangerous it is? We can't afford to let Sophie get to the jewels again, after what happened last time!" James protested, introducing himself as he did.

"James, they sound quite reasonable to me. If we don't try to defeat Queen Sophie now, we might never... ever... have a chance to save Fantasia again. James, you know that if we don't take the risk now, when we try in the future, we won't be able to defeat Queen Sophie at all, because of her rising power. Please, forget what happened last time and let's help them now. I, Talia Andrews, am devoting myself to helping Lizzie and Pearl save Fantasia at any cost!" Talia announced.

“I, Daniel Bone, will help everyone save Fantasia so that freedom and justice can prevail! By the way, James, Talia is right, according to my calculations. It is best to take the risk and save Fantasia, then to just let Queen Sophie take over everything and you know that my facts and statistics are always right” Daniel added, agreeing with Talia in an attempt to try and convince James to help them.

James sighed. He knew it was useless to protest. “Fine, I’ll help too. But only because you guys want me to, okay?” he told them.

Lizzie decided to interrupt the conversation. “It’s great that everyone agrees to help, but could someone at least tell me what happened last time? I seem to be the only one who has no idea at all” she asked politely, but with a clear hint of annoyance in her voice.

“Sorry Lizzie, I forgot to explain. Let me start from the beginning. Talia was more attached to her jewel than the others. James and Daniel had jewel wearers in their families, so it was alright for them to be seen wearing the jewel at home. Talia was given her jewel by Orchidia Browne, one of your Gran’s friends. Talia could not be seen with the jewel by anyone other than James and Mrs. Browne. She could never take it off” Pearl began.

"Wait... so you're saying that Orchidia Browne, as in Mrs. Browne next door, used to wear a JEWEL! That is awesome. No wonder she was so suspicious the other day!" Lizzie exclaimed happily, understanding what Pearl had explained to her so far.

"So basically, when Queen Sophie took away our jewels, Talia didn't yet know how to cope without her jewel because she had never taken it off. All her strength was gone, and she could barely breathe or move at all. It was a terrible time to see my best friend suffer like that" James continued, telling the tragic tale.

"But after a while, I learned how to manage, right James? Everything turned out just fine and I'm still alive. Really, James, don't exaggerate and worry too much. You'll just turn into a big mess at the end!" Talia said, chuckling to herself.

"Whatever you say, T!" James agreed, making a silly face.

Everyone laughed, all quite amused by James. They all enjoyed the relaxing moment for a few seconds before they were brought back to reality. "Time for you three to transform!" Pearl announced, grabbing James's jewel from Lizzie's hands.

Pearl walked over to James and freed him from the chains. James then wore the amber jewel on his little ring. Lizzie could see the worried expression on his face. He was scared for Talia.

"You seem to be concerned about everything that involves Talia, James. Is anything wrong?" Pearl asked gently.

James looked down and sighed. "I always wonder if Talia considers me as her best friend. I keep on trying to show her how much I care for our friendship, but she doesn't ever change, not at all" he confessed, seeming quite upset.

"The time will come when Talia shows you her true response. For now, just transform and help us defeat Queen Sophie, alright?" Pearl told James, trying her best to cheer him up.

James nodded. He too chanted the magic words and soon he was wearing an amber-colored suit with elaborate golden swirls all over. He also held a sturdy, long rope with a handle, in which his jewel was carefully fitted. By then everyone had transformed, and they were ready for their ambush.

Suddenly, they all heard an evil cackle echo in the room. "I heard that someone has been looking for me, am I right? Ahahahahaha! Fools, you're all ridiculous fools!" the voice said, cackling in a cold, gravelly tone that sounded quite familiar to all five allies. Strangely familiar…

A NEW HERO

"Queen Sophie! What brings you here?" Pearl asked politely, but her voice had a cold tone to it.

Sophie cackled, her voice echoing in the damp, dark room. "Why, I was just about to ask you the same thing, my dear friends!" she teased, an evil smirk visible on her face.

Everyone looked at her, not amused. "Don't even think about playing your little games of innocence, you lying snob!" Pearl angrily exclaimed.

Lizzie was in complete agreement with Pearl. They weren't going to let the Queen off that easily. My friends and I have everything and everyone against you, so we'll either do this the easy way or not" Lizzie told her strictly, supporting Pearl to confront the Queen properly.

"Well, I'm doing this the way I want, which is where I end up becoming the most powerful person in the world! And none of you will ever be able to stop me from living my dream, never!" Sophie indignantly screeched, scowling at all five of the allies in front of her.

Lizzie, Pearl, James, Daniel, and Talia exchanged glances. They had all hoped that it wouldn't have to come to a point where they had to battle Queen Sophie, but now there was nothing they could do about it. All five of them had to fight for Fantasia and everything it meant.

"Then I'm sure you won't mind a little bit of a battle, will you?" Lizzie asked politely with a sheepish grin plastered on her face.

Queen Sophie stepped forward. "Precisely, I won't. If I win, you all give up your jewels. If you win, I'll do what you say. Deal?" she asked confidently.

Lizzie didn't even hesitate to think at all. "You're on, Sophie. But I wouldn't be too confident if I were you, alright?" she agreed, warning Queen Sophie, just to mess with her.

Sophie smirked mischievously. "Guards! I need you down here, NOW!" she yelled. Lizzie and the others started to giggle. Queen Sophie had no idea that everyone working in the palace had gone to join the rebellion with Betty. Noticing the laughter, Sophie snapped "Why are you all laughing? You will regret it when my guards come and destroy all of you!".

"As if! You don't have anyone to help you anymore, Sophie. They all left you and joined our forces. You're on your own now" Pearl said, scoffing.

Sophie was quite impressed by how far the allies had come. "You've managed to do all that? Well done, I must say" she told the allies.

"Don't try to stall, Sophie. Let's get this over with and afterward, you will see that the allies are far better than you. We can all promise you that for sure!" Talia stated, bringing more enthusiasm to the group. Sophie was getting annoyed by how the allies had improved their strategies. She noticed a slight change in their team, a new jewel holder.

"Who is this new young lady in Betty Thomas's suit? I demand to know!" Sophie insisted.

"First of all, it's not her suit, it's mine. Secondly, I am Lizzie Thomas, the new holder of the red ruby. Anyway, I thought you knew who I was" Lizzie said, stepping forward to introduce herself.

"I already knew that you were Betty's granddaughter! I just needed you to confirm that for me before I knew that I was 100% right" Sophie snapped.

"Anyways, you're all lame. I mean, how do you expect to defeat me, the Queen of Fantasia with your little, useless jewels? If you think that you can win against me, you have no idea how stupid you are!" she continued, chuckling rudely.

“Don’t even think about it, Sophie. You haven’t heard about something called teamwork” Daniel pointed out.

“Why do I want to know about that nonsense when I have all kinds of power in my hands! With that I could easily destroy your useless teamwork!” Sophie stated, cackling once again.

Everyone could see that Lizzie was fuming. Sophie had gone too far. Lizzie burst into the air angrily, aiming large lightning bolts at the Queen. Everyone stared at her in utmost shock, including Sophie. The allies were quite pleased, especially Pearl. She had known all along that Lizzie was the right person to use the red ruby and the appearance of Lizzie’s powers had proven it.

Even Lizzie herself was surprised by the fact that she had been able to activate her powers at all. “Without Pearl and everyone else who helped me believe in myself and this mission, I probably would never have made it so far,” Lizzie thought, making a mental note to thank everyone later.

But their moment of pleasure came to an end when Sophie pulled out a bag from nowhere. She had harvested pixie dust, taking all of the reserves of the poor pixies living in the dungeons. Sophie hastily started to sprinkle the glittering dust around her. Pearl, Talia, Daniel, and James used their powers to fly and join Lizzie, who had stopped shooting lightning bolts for the moment. They were finally ready to free Fantasia from the evil clutches of the White Queen, together.

Sophie had created an army of soldiers, all armed with metal swords and shields. "En Garde, my soldiers! Attack them! Don't let them lay a single hand on you!" She ordered them. The soldiers rushed forward at the allies, forcing them to fight back. As Lizzie was dodging one of the soldier's swords, her staff lightly brushed the shield in front of her, making the soldier and his weapons vanish into thin air. Lizzie immediately understood what Sophie was doing. She was tricking them by creating illusions for them to fight against!

"Everyone! These soldiers are illusions! We need to touch every single one of them so that they disappear!" Lizzie shouted, warning the others about the illusioned soldiers.

All five of them dashed around, making sure that they removed every illusion from view. Within a matter of a few minutes, all the soldiers had disappeared, leaving Queen Sophie as their only opponent. However, Queen Sophie had many more tricks up her sleeve. She once again sprinkled pixie dust all over the room, and a few seconds later, the walls and ceiling were covered in thick sheets of ice.

James saw what Sophie was trying to do. He hollered "So this is the game you want to play, Sophie? Then let's play it!".

THE END OF THE WHITE QUEEN

The allies easily defended themselves against the little ice trick of Sophie's. Talia easily unfroze the walls with fire, making a large puddle of water on the floor. Queen Sophie used her powers and created a handful of obstacles, but the allies always stopped her by using their powers against her. Eventually, the allies decided to attack Sophie instead of letting her put them in harm's way.

James and Pearl merged their powers and crafted an indestructible cage, to trap Sophie by using her tactics. Lizzie, Daniel, and Talia took care of luring Sophie into the cage. They put together their powers and created a voice, sounding like Lizzie. Then all five of them quickly hid away in different corners of the room, getting ready for the exact moment where Queen Sophie would fall into their trap.

"Alright, Queen Sophie, we give up! We will give you our jewels and you can rule the entire world" the fake voice of Lizzie confessed, just loud enough so that Sophie lost her concentration while casting another spell with her pixie dust. Sophie turned around, slowly walking over to the place she heard the voice from.

The fake voice led Sophie to the cage. She pulled open the heavy metal door and walked in. "Hand me your jewels, now! I will finally be able to rule the world like I always wanted to and there won't be anyone else to ever stop me! My power will reach no limit, and you five will be nothing, nothing at all!" Sophie said, ordering the allies to listen to her.

At that moment Pearl came out of hiding and slammed the cage door shut, making a loud thud. Sophie looked around to see what the noise was, only to find out that she had been tricked. She screamed in rage, her yells echoing noisily in the room. Lizzie and the other allies left their hiding spots, joining Pearl in front of the cage.

"I think it isn't you who will win today, Sophie! Justice will prevail in all of Fantasia, and you will go where you belong, in the dungeons!" Daniel shouted, telling Sophie about her now obvious fate.

"I still have one way to defeat you! I won't let any of you ruin this for me, especially you, Lizzie!" Sophie bellowed furiously.

The allies looked around for anything Queen Sophie could use to defeat them, but they couldn't see anything of possible danger to them. What they didn't know was that Queen Sophie had her weapon with her. As the five tried their best to find out what Sophie had in store for them, the Queen pulled out her pixie dust bag, silently sprinkling it all over herself. James noticed out of the corner of his eye that Sophie was using her pixie dust. "She is always up to no good, isn't she?" he wondered.

James quietly used his power, so that Queen Sophie wouldn't notice him and a few seconds later, the bag of pixie dust was in his grasp. Sophie had put on quite a frustrated expression on her face. "Look everyone, I believe this is what we are looking for. It was with Sophie the whole time!" James cried out, snapping with his fingers to catch the other allies' attention. Pearl, Lizzie, Daniel, and Talia turned around to see what James was talking about. There they saw the small bag of pixie dust that Queen Sophie had brought with her earlier.

"Of course! The pixie dust was the only thing Sophie could have used to defeat us because it can create anything she wants!" Talia exclaimed in understanding.

"You had no right to take my belongings away from me! How did you even get to it when it was with me in this horrible cage the whole time?" Sophie yelled, fussing over her bag.

"That's true... How did you even get to her bag, James? I hope you didn't go inside the cage or something, just to take away Sophie's bag of pixie dust..." Lizzie asked curiously.

Everyone was very interested to know how James had managed to pull off such a trick. "I just used my power and brought it into a situation from a dream I had. It was honestly easy to do it silently because I don't need my voice to use my powers, you see" James explained, telling everyone how he had so quickly taken away Sophie's bag of pixie dust from her.

"That makes sense! Well, it's great that we have Queen Sophie's pixie dust, and we can use it to our advantage!" Pearl pointed out.

"Hmm... And I think I probably might just have the right idea to do exactly that." Daniel said, mischievously rubbing his hands.

Everyone looked at Daniel, waiting for a response. He didn't understand that everybody was waiting for him. A minute later, no one could stand to wait any longer. "JUST TELL US YOUR IDEA!" the other allies yelled impatiently at Daniel.

Daniel pushed everyone, moving them away from the cage. The allies knew that it was to protect their plans from Sophie and her evil ideas. “Why don’t we get more proof to expose Queen Sophie? After all, the more people we can convince, the better! We should use the pixie dust to cast a spell that will force Queen Sophie to say only the truth. Once we find out everything, we can easily reveal the terrible plans of the White Queen” Daniel explained, once he felt that he had taken everyone far enough from the cage.

“Oh! Then we can capture the whole scene to show all of Fantasia, or even better, let everyone hear Queen Sophie live at the palace gates! Wonderful!” Pearl exclaimed, catching on to Daniel’s idea. Lizzie, Talia, and James all nodded in agreement.

“I think we should hurry now... Before that evil genius of a Queen does something else to change our plans. Let’s get this party started!” Lizzie announced, bringing up her hand for a team high-five.

REALITY EXPOSED

The five allies set up their plan to expose Queen Sophie. Daniel and James snuck up behind Sophie's cage and knocked her out with Daniel's weapon, a magnifying glass tied to James's rope, whilst the girls quickly dashed around and sprinkled the pixie dust all over Sophie and the cage. All five of them stepped back to look at their work. Just then the allies heard a loud crowd passing by who were protesting, most probably against Queen Sophie.

"Perfect timing! Let's cast the spell!" Pearl exclaimed cheerfully, clapping her hands together, feeling very excited about their plan.

"Repeat after me; Only a true response each time, nothing to lie or mime" Daniel instructed. The allies knew that Daniel had used his powers to learn pixie magic, so they were sure that they could trust his instructions to cast the spell.

Everyone repeated Daniel's sentence in chorus. A few seconds later, a magical, glittery light appeared all around Sophie. Her eyes turned from its cold blue to a glowing shade of green. She then stood up inside the cage, standing straight and still like a robot. The allies looked at Sophie in amazement. They were all quite surprised about the fact that the spell they cast using the pixie dust had done something.

"Let's see if the spell works since that's the one thing that we don't even know. Pearl, why don't you try and ask her a question that you already know the true answer to?" Daniel asked.

Pearl nodded. She quickly paused to think of a simple question. A few moments later, Pearl walked over to the cage and questioned "Did you kill your father by slicing his head off?".

Sophie answered almost immediately. "Yes, I did kill my father by slicing off his head," she said to them loud and clear in response.

Everyone watched in excitement. The allies were all relieved that their spell had worked, and now they could easily expose Queen Sophie to the world. Everyone decided to ask a few funny questions for Sophie to answer, just to pass the time a little. After they all had a good laugh, Daniel created a teleportation portal, which would lead them straight to the rebellion in front of the palace. It was finally the time to end the reign of the White Queen once and for all.

Everybody stepped into the portal one by one until only Daniel and James were left to carry Queen Sophie and the cage into the portal. A minute later, they all landed in the middle of the rebellion's path. As the large group of people got closer and closer, they noticed the allies and the cage. "OH MY GOD! Look everyone, the allies have returned to us!" one of the creatures in the crowd yelled loudly in excitement.

"Hello, dear Fantasian citizens! We all promised you justice, and here it is, live for you to see!" Pearl spoke, loud and clear through a microphone, producing it using her powers.

"What about the cage? Could you explain what it is?" another creature asked.

The crowded group was uncontrollably crazy, from people shouting and screaming, demanding answers to questions, and to the whole rebellion going wild in excitement. The allies were suddenly panicked. How could they possibly get such a crowd to listen to them? Luckily, Betty came to help at the right time. "EVERYONE CALM DOWN! I WANT PINDROP SILENCE NOW!" Betty roared at the rebellion, restoring order to everything.

Not a single person dared to even let a sound out of them because no one wanted to see Betty in her angry state. Lizzie thankfully smiled over at her grandmother, who just smiled back warmly. "In this cage, we have Queen Sophie, whom we've cast a spell on. She will now only speak the truth, which is what will bring us to justice. It's about time that we let everyone know about Sophie's terrible schemes" Lizzie explained, watching out to make sure that there wasn't a single person who was not paying attention to her.

The crowd was stunned. No one in the history of Fantasia had ever been able to bring such a powerful person to justice. Once the people had finished asking their queries and questions, the allies decided to tell everyone about everything that they had originally found out before battling Queen Sophie.

"To begin with, I'm pretty sure that everyone knows that Queen Sophie made an announcement at her dinner party at Rodney's. She was going to clone herself. But nobody knew how or why. The way and the reasons why Sophie was planning to clone herself were brutal and cruel. We, the allies know the whole backstory to the terrible plans of 9the White Queen, but for all of you to understand everything, it would be best if we let Sophie herself do the explaining" Daniel started, telling the rebellion more about the horrible doings of Queen Sophie.

"Didn't she say that she wanted to have a successor to her throne? Wasn't that the real reason she wanted to clone herself?" people from the rebellion crowd queried questioningly.

"Queen Sophie, what did you really intend to do by cloning yourself and how did you even plan to clone yourself in the first place?" James asked, ignoring the questions from the crowd.

Once again, Sophie immediately responded to James's question. "I intended to take over all the kingdoms in the world, not to have an heir to my throne. I figured out that if I had lots of pixie dust, I could cast a powerful spell to create a perfect clone of myself and that too multiple times. Firstly, I captured pixies and forced them to produce pixie dust for me. Today I had planned to make the first clone in front of everyone and create the rest of them in my secret room. After that, I was going to send my clones to take over all the countries and kingdoms that exist so that the whole universe would belong to me!" she answered in detail.

All the people who had just heard Queen Sophie telling everyone her evil plans were astonished. They had no idea that Sophie had such horrible things in mind. The crowd angrily shouted rudely at Sophie and threw rotten food at her. Again Betty had to command everyone to calm down.

Once everyone had once again quieted down, Lizzie cleared her throat and asked the crowd "Now that you all know the truth, we all need you to tell us, should we throw Queen Sophie into the dungeons, or not?".

A MAGICAL END

"Of course, to the dungeons! There is nothing better to do with such a terrible person other than throwing them into the dungeons!" someone from the rebellion shouted angrily, responding to Lizzie's question.

A few other people in the crowd shouted in agreement. Eventually, there was a loud chant going on amongst the rebellion. They chanted "To the dungeons, to the dungeons, to the dungeons!" again and again, getting noisier and noisier each time. However, there was one person at the very center of the crowd who had been trying to speak in the midst of all the chaos. Lizzie, being the only one who had noticed the person trying to speak, used her powers to fly above the people and land exactly in the middle.

The person who had been trying to talk was an old man, who was using a little wooden cane to stand. Lizzie carefully picked up the old man and brought him over to the others. The old man was confused. "Why did you do that? I was perfectly fine where I was" the old man asked, confused by Lizzie.

"Well sir, I thought I heard you trying to say something, but no one seemed to listen. I feel that you have something important to say, so I thought that you might want a little bit of help so that you could be heard. That's why I brought you over here" Lizzie explained to him.

"Why thank you, young lady! Although I do wonder how you plan to take control of such a wild crowd..."

Lizzie nodded over to her Gran, who put her thumbs up for Lizzie to know. Lizzie's Gran walked over to the front of the crowd and screeched deafeningly "STOP THAT RIGHT THIS SECOND!".

The crowd turned silent. The old man was in shock. He couldn't stop staring at Lizzie. Lizzie just placed her hand on the old man's shoulder and whispered to him "Tell them, tell everyone what you think".

"Firstly, my name is Jack. Now, I want to answer the question of whether we should send Queen Sophie to the dungeons or not" the old man began, introducing himself to the rebellion.

Many people in the crowd murmured in disbelief. The allies smiled and nodded encouragingly. "As we all know, most of you want Queen Sophie to be imprisoned in the dungeons. However, I disagree with all of you. Even if someone isn't the best of the best, even if they are a terrible person, they deserve a second chance. Why? All good people make mistakes, and will always learn from them, but they can only do so if given the chance to learn. A good, kind human left to be free is far better than an evil, cruel human chained up and locked away. I hope you all understand and make the right choice for this poor soul" Jack finished, leaving the entire group of people who had gathered at the palace in amazement.

The crowd was silent. Most people had no idea of what they wanted to do with Sophie. Lizzie and the allies were tense, given that they had left the decision of Queen Sophie's fate to the citizens of Fantasia. Lizzie believed Jack, not just because she knew he was right, but because she felt a strong connection that just made her want to believe Jack more than ever.

Suddenly, someone in the crowd began to speak. "I agree with Jack. Queen Sophie is a human being, and she deserves a second chance like the rest of us!" the person said.

Lizzie was relieved. At least someone believed Jack! Just as Lizzie was about to ask her Gran about what to do, since almost no one was answering, another creature shouted out "Let's give Queen Sophie another chance!". Many other people nodded understandingly and one by one, they started to shout in agreement with Jack.

Soon enough, the entire rebellion had begun to chant for giving Sophie another chance. The allies were overjoyed. justice would be brought to Fantasia and Queen Sophie would now change, for good!

"Alright, everyone! It's time we bring Fantasia to justice and give Queen Sophie's soul another chance!" The allies happily announced to the crowd.

Everyone whooped and cheered as the allies stood together in a circle near the cage. One by one, Talia, Daniel, James, Pearl, and Lizzie called out their powers, ready to use. "Time for some teamwork!" Lizzie yelled to the others enthusiastically.

All the five allies put their hands in the middle. A few seconds later, a bright swirl of colorful light burst out into the air and enclosed the cage in which Queen Sophie was held. The crowd watched eagerly, engrossed by the magical scene in front of them. Suddenly, the swirl of light flashed brightly, forcing everyone to close their eyes.

Once everyone opened their eyes, the cage was no longer there. In place of it was Sophie and shockingly, her father, King Marcus, standing beside her. Sophie looked different. She no longer wore the cold, evil look on her face. Instead, it was replaced by a cheerful, happy expression. The entire rebellion was overjoyed to see King Marcus returning to Fantasia's throne, with a new, changed Princess Sophie at his side.

"Dear people of Fantasia, I am glad to be back with you today. I will step back to my place as King, with my lovely daughter, Princess Sophie there to help me take care of the kingdom. Now Fantasia is free from any evil burdens and we can all live in harmony!" King Marcus announced, making the crowd erupt in happy cheer.

Betty decided that she would hand her advisor position to Jack. She too had felt a strong connection between her and Jack, and Betty felt that King Marcus needed him more than he needed her. Betty would be returning to the farm, along with Lizzie. Lizzie and Betty wanted their family to know about the wonderful realm of Fantasia, now that the danger was gone forever.

Just as the allies had de-transformed and returned to the front of the palace, Diego, Flutter, and Dwarfer ran over to them. "Lizzie! We're so glad to see you! Thanks to you and your great ideas, Fantasia is now back to how it was!" Flutter squealed in excitement.

Lizzie shook her head. She replied to Flutter "No, it wasn't me. It was all of us, working as a team. We would have never got through this adventure without each other".

Special Credits

Lawrence Mayaki - Mentor and Foreword

Diti Manchanda - Illustration

Parthasarathy and Rebecca Pickering - Reviewing Content

ACKNOWLEDGEMENTS

I would like to thank my family, especially my Dad for encouraging and supporting me in the process of this book.

I am very grateful to my friends, particularly Manasvi, Shambhavi and Shruti for giving me a lot of motivation whilst I was writing this book.

I am also very thankful to my primary school teachers; Ms. Allen, Ms. Chiodo, and Mr. Mayaki who have been my mentors in my writing journey.

Special thanks to Mr. Mayaki for helping me improve my writing

Special thanks to Parthasarathy Uncle for being supportive and advising me in this adventure

Special thanks to my friend Diti for illustrating and making it an even more magical experience

And finally, thank you, dear Readers, for reading along with Lizzie and her remarkable journey.

ABOUT THE AUTHOR

Priyankha Kamalakannan is a keen reader, writer, and creative thinker living in Germany. Her passion for literature is what brought her to write her first book. Priyankha likes to devote a lot of time and effort whenever it comes to writing or reading. She also connects a lot of her life to writing, such as her Ted talk, her website, her YouTube channel, and participation in external events. However, she mostly loves spending time with friends and family.

Email: priyankha.itsme@gmail.com
Ted Talk: The Power of Writing | Priyankha Kamalakannan | TEDxYouth@TFIS
Website: http://www.priyankhakamal.com/
YouTube Channel: Priyankha K

www.ingramcontent.com/pod-product-compliance
Lightning Source LLC
LaVergne TN
LVHW091146150826
845672LV00005B/1058

* 9 7 9 8 7 6 0 3 2 3 0 9 5 *